Kate had never felt this way in her life. She could hardly believe these exquisite sensations. Laura removed her lips from Kate's mouth to trace around one erect nipple, circling it with her tongue, then the other, exploring and tasting. With a tiny cry, Kate moved under Laura. She felt a sudden painful rush of desire and her wetness increased.

"Oh, Laura..." she breathed. Laura reached down with one hand and stroked the silky skin on the inside of Kate's thighs. Kate was in agony. She needed Laura's more intimate touch. She couldn't wait any longer. She moved her hips in invitation. Laura planted kisses down across her stomach, tiny electrifying strokes of her tongue. Then her mouth found the silky wet place Kate was aching for her to taste. Kate gasped, arching her hips as Laura's stroking sent her into a fever.

This was a whole new experience for Kate. Her previous unsatisfactory experiences with a man hadn't included this kind of sensual intimacy, and she'd never in all of her fantasies about women, particularly about Laura, ever imagined it could feel like this. She was floating above herself, her whole body seemed to be filled with honey, and only her hips moved slightly in rhythm with Laura's strokes.

For Helen
Whose love makes everything possible

Ann O'Leary

THE NAIAD PRESS, INC.
1997

Copyright © 1997 by Ann O'Leary

All rights reserved. No part of this book may be reproduced or transmitted in any form or by any means, electronic or mechanical, including photocopying, without permission in writing from the publisher.

Printed in the United States of America on acid-free paper
First Edition

Editor: Christine Cassidy
Cover designer: Bonnie Liss (Phoenix Graphics)
Typesetter: Sandi Stancil

Library of Congress Cataloging-in-Publication Data

O'Leary, Ann, 1955 –
  Letting go / by Ann O'Leary.
     p.   cm.
  ISBN 1-56280-183-X (pbk.)
  I. Title.
PR9619.3.O386L48   1997
823'.54—dc21   97-10006
                                                                  CIP

CHAPTER ONE

It was a hot summer's night in Melbourne, silent and still except for the constant soothing chirps of the crickets. Laura's apartment was bathed in moonlight, which indiscriminately cast its ghostly wash over objects here and there. Part of a renovated Art Deco building on the Saint Kilda Beach foreshore, the apartment was not large, but exuded a feeling of spaciousness and light. It consisted of a bedroom with bathroom on a mezzanine level that created a lower ceiling downstairs over about one third of the area. Under this was a kitchen and laundry, and a small

TV and office space. The rest of the space downstairs was open to the vaulted ceiling and one could enjoy a clear view of the sea from both levels, through soaring glass windows. The mezzanine floor was supported by simple round columns, and its edge, like the kitchen bench directly beneath it, was rounded to mirror the curved deco balcony which extended the full width of the apartment. The furniture was modern, but classical in style. The color scheme was soft greens, teal and white that reflected the sea view.

The heat was oppressive, steamy. On the balcony, leaning back in a deck chair, Laura was sitting alone. She was wearing a light silk robe. One leg was drawn up, with her heel resting on the edge of the chair. Her exposed thigh was smooth and tanned a light golden brown, and the soft robe had slipped off one shoulder, partly revealing her breasts. She didn't care that it was two-thirty in the morning, and she had been sitting here alone for some time. Long enough to drink half a bottle of cognac and smoke most of a pack of cigarettes. The ashtray on the table beside her was overflowing, and she was feeling decidedly woozy. But she had waited this long, and she would continue to wait until Debbie finally came home.

She had lived with Debbie for nearly three years, and things had not been going well in recent months. Their relationship had never recovered from Debbie's affair a year ago. Laura felt like she had tried to forgive her, but things were never the same. Laura's closest friends had advised her then to walk away. Mostly they'd never liked Debbie much, with her spoiled-child attitude and affectations. Some considered her a bimbo. Despite this, Laura had hung on, reluctant to give up on this relationship she thought she badly needed. Debbie came into her life at a time when Laura had emotionally hit rock-bottom. She'd had two years of being alone after the death of Alexandra, the one true love of her life, two years of shutting everyone out. A few sordid one-night stands the only degree of intimacy she'd been able to endure. She was deeply immersed in her work, getting her newly formed agency together, desperately trying to fill the huge empty hole inside her. Debbie, aged twenty-eight, full of fun and vitality, made Laura feel alive again. She set her sights on Laura and eventually succeeded in seducing her, easing a lot of Laura's heartache. Laura just let it all happen because she knew she couldn't go on the way she had been. She'd thought she was ready for a relationship again.

Before long Debbie moved in with her and they'd been quite happy for a couple of years. Laura never loved Debbie the way she had loved Alexandra. She didn't expect that. It wasn't possible to be that deeply in love with anyone else.

Once again, she was plagued by suspicions. Debbie was so distant lately. She was hardly ever home, always working late, and impatiently avoiding Laura's questions. Laura didn't want to believe it. Hadn't Debbie promised it wouldn't happen again? But all the signs were there. Laura had considered the situation for some time and decided at last to face the truth. Whatever love she once had for Debbie was gone. Debbie was making a fool of her, and as far as Laura was concerned, the relationship was over. But she wasn't going to let Debbie off lightly.

She was angry, determined to confront her tonight and demand the truth.

Suddenly out of the darkness, headlights flashed across Laura's face. One of the few cars purring along the beach road below turned into the driveway that ran alongside the block of six apartments, and it glided up the steep driveway to the garages at the back. It was two-forty. Debbie had at last arrived home.

Laura continued to sit quietly, staring out toward the sea. A ray of moonlight fell across her arm as she reached for yet another cigarette. The cold knot in her stomach tightened its grip and her heart began to thud in trepidation. She waited until she heard the key turn in the lock, then slowly rose and went inside, standing in the shadows by the wide French doors.

Laura watched Debbie sneak in. She removed her black patent high-heeled shoes, obviously trying to avoid making any noise on the parquetry floor. Laura admired, not for the first time, Debbie's legs. Her smart business suit revealed her shapely hips and the tight top under her open jacket showed off her full breasts. She placed her briefcase carefully on the floor while she turned to lock the door. The keys slipped out of her hand to the floor with a small clatter.

"Shit," she muttered as she bent quickly to retrieve them. Laura took a deep drag of her cigarette, and Debbie jumped. "Jesus Christ, Laura, what the hell are you doing there? You scared me half to death!" She took a few steps closer, moving cautiously, as if steeling herself for a confrontation.

She fingered the pendant around her neck, sliding it back and forth along its chain.

Laura, her voice thick with anger, brandy and cigarettes, said, "I've been waiting for you for hours. Where've you been? It's a quarter to three."

"I told you I had to work late. There was an important litigation case to prepare for." Debbie's tone sounded defensive even to her own ears. She hoped her confident façade was masking her growing fear. Her hands felt sweaty.

She came inside and removed her jacket, tossing it casually over a chair. Moonlight splashed across her face. She tossed her shoulder-length blonde hair in that manner Laura had always found so sexy. If she could just put her arms around Laura, hold her close and kiss her neck, the way Laura liked, she could probably save this situation. She could usually get around her that way. She noticed Laura fiddling with the ring on her left middle finger, twisting it around in an agitated fashion.

Debbie gave a seductive smile and said, "Won't you hold me, honey? I'm really tired and I just want to go to bed."

But Laura's cold unwavering gaze remained a barrier between them. Laura took another long draw on her cigarette and turned away. She stood on the threshold of the open French doors and looked out into the darkness.

"Who is she, Debbie? I know you're seeing someone and I just want to know who she is."

Debbie panicked; the situation was slipping out of her control. "Don't be ridiculous, honey! I've been working! You know I've got to be there when they need me. What am I supposed to say when my boss asks me to work late? 'Oh I'm sorry, but I can't because my girlfriend develops jealous fantasies if I'm not home on time'? You know the legal business is very competitive and if I don't give the firm one hundred and fifty percent, they're not likely to find me a position when I finish my degree, are they?" Laura didn't reply, and Debbie felt she'd gained some ground. She added sweetly, "You want me to do well, don't you, honey?"

Debbie was ambitious and worked hard. She was studying part-time for her law degree and working as personal assistant to the senior partner of a large law firm. Laura said she didn't have a problem with occasional long working hours; it happened quite a lot in her own business.

"There's no law firm I ever heard of that works half the fucking night as often as yours does, just preparing ordinary cases. That's bullshit, Debbie. So tell me, where were you?" She spoke in a monotone. She clearly wasn't going to crack.

Debbie had already noticed the odor of alcohol, and she could see the bottle and glass on the outdoor table. She jumped to the offensive. She raised her voice and spoke to Laura's straight back — like a brick wall, she thought. "You're half drunk, Laura. There's no point in continuing this conversation tonight. I'm going to bed." With that, she turned and grabbed her jacket from the chair, picked up her briefcase and started up the black iron winding staircase to their bedroom. She badly wanted a shower.

Laura raised her voice to Debbie's retreating

shadow. "I rang you. I rang your direct line. I rang your boss's direct line and the main office number. I rang at nine o'clock, ten o'clock, midnight and again at one. You weren't there, Debbie." Her voice caught on those last words as she stifled a sob.

Debbie froze. A cold chill crept up her spine. Further lies would be a waste of time. Laura wasn't going to forgive her this time. It was over. Defeated and angry, she spat out her last confession. "All right, Laura. I've been having an affair. You really want to know who it is? Well, I hope you're ready for this." She paused, watching Laura's silhouette in the doorway; she hadn't moved. She felt dread as she imagined the impact of what she was about to say. She clenched her fists and drew in a deep breath. "It's Mark Downing."

Laura looked like she would faint. There was an awful silence filled only by the constant drone of the crickets in the background. She slowly stepped over to the sofa and sank down safely in the cushions before she found her voice. It was barely above a whisper. "You've been screwing a man? I don't believe it! You're a lesbian. Since when have you been interested in men? All this time... while you've been living with me..." Her voice trailed off.

Debbie felt the need to try to justify herself, even if it was a waste of time. "For God's sake, Laura, I'm not the first woman to fuck her boss for the sake of her career. Okay, it's not a great thing to do, but in the legal business, women need as much help as they can get." She stood there on the stairs waiting for Laura to respond. Laura drew her knees up under her chin and hugged them tightly as if trying to disappear into a tiny ball.

A few moments passed before Laura spoke again, in a measured tone. "I want you out of my house by tomorrow night. I want all of your things out of here, and then I never want to see you again. For as long as you live." Dry-eyed, she was clearly shell-shocked.

Debbie stomped up the stairs, and Laura heard the bathroom door slam. She remained on the sofa with her head on her knees and allowed the tears to flow freely. She rocked herself gently, trying to soothe the horrible ache in her chest. It was worse than she had imagined. How could she have so blindly misjudged Debbie's character, and why had she allowed this pretense of a relationship to drag on for so long? She stretched out on the sofa. Finally, around four o'clock, with the help of the brandy she'd consumed earlier, she drifted off to sleep.

CHAPTER TWO

Laura awoke with a start. She sat up and held her pounding head. Her eyes were glued together and her mouth tasted terrible. Debbie was clattering about in the kitchen, just out of her sight.

Not wanting to see or speak with her this morning, she rose from the sofa and headed upstairs as quickly as she could, given the cramp in her leg. She locked the bathroom door behind her and inspected the damage in the mirror. She didn't look good. Her eyes were red and puffy, and her face was blotchy. Thank God someone invented makeup, she thought.

As she reached into the cupboard under the vanity basin for the mouthwash, she saw her watch lying on the bench. It was eight-thirty. She remembered with a jolt that today was Friday and she and her business partner, Tony, had a new-business presentation to make this morning. Her pulse quickened; she felt panicky, disoriented. How was she going to get through it? Her head was throbbing, and she couldn't even think straight. She consoled herself slightly with the thought that the meeting wasn't until eleven o'clock. Thank God. She had some time to get her act together. She gargled until her mouth was burning, then attacked her teeth vigorously with her toothbrush. With relief, she heard the front door slam as she turned on the shower. She could relax a little, now that Debbie had left, but she would have to hurry. She started to feel almost human again as the hot water surged over her. She didn't have time to dwell on the events of last night now. She needed to concentrate as best she could on the job she had to do today.

In her dressing-room, she selected an outfit for this morning's presentation. She chose a cream linen suit with a fitted skirt finishing a few inches above the knee, and a plain long-line jacket. It buttoned up high enough that she didn't have to wear a shirt under it, and it looked good against her golden skin. She added a simple gold chain around her throat and small gold earrings. She slid her stockinged feet into black high-heeled court shoes and stepped across to the mirror to survey her appearance. Apart from the makeup, which could wait until she got to the office, she looked presentable. She ran her hands through her short dark hair and sighed wearily. She had a challenging day ahead of her, and she'd be struggling to get through it. She put on her watch and the rings she always wore, then headed downstairs.

As she gulped down a couple of painkillers with a strong coffee, she considered how fortunate she was to have a partner like Tony. On a day like this when she was feeling less than dynamic, she knew she could rely on him to fill in the gaps and help maintain her humor. As she locked her apartment and headed off to her lovingly restored old Mercedes in the garage, she remembered with a smile something Tony often said to her: "I'm telling you, mate, it's your bloody looks that win us these clients, not our talent. That's what matters in the end to these bastards. I'd be stuffed without you — Christ knows, I've got a face like a monkey's arse!"

The business was called Adworks. Laura and Tony had previously worked together for many years on some important accounts in a large international agency. Laura felt relaxed and comfortable with him and he was one hell of an account director. She liked his infectious enthusiasm and energy. He was quick-witted and down to earth. He called a spade a "fuckin' shovel."

Laura had been a group-creative director when Tony approached her nearly three years ago with the idea of forming a partnership. Laura realized it was just the opportunity she'd been waiting for. She was thirty-six then and tired of working for other people. She knew she and Tony could work well together and that he would make a trustworthy partner. It had been very hard work for some time, but business now was good and the hours were more regular these days. They hired in freelance people to write copy and to help with ideas and layouts when necessary. The only permanent staff they required was an assistant to help in many areas, including phone-answering, typing, and looking after clients when they arrived for meetings. Unfortunately, a woman who'd been in this position since they started had left recently to travel overseas. She'd been wonderful and their attempts to replace her had so far been unsuccessful. Being without an assistant during their current busy period was making life difficult.

Their office was small, located in a modern office building in a fashionable inner suburb of Melbourne. Laura thought again as she climbed the one flight of stairs to Adworks that she really must make the time next week when things quieted down to find an assistant. She realized with irritation that she would have to, apart from many more important things, prepare the boardroom and organize coffee for this morning's meeting. Tony never remembered those details.

She was totally surprised then, as she stepped through the doorway, to see a young woman, perhaps eighteen years old, sitting behind the reception desk. Her head was down and she was leafing through a magazine. Laura stopped in her tracks, wondering who on earth she could be, when a large pink balloon of bubble gum began to slowly protrude from the woman's mouth. It reached an enormous size before bursting with a loud crack, and was then sucked in again to prepare for the next bubble. Laura cleared her throat and approached the desk.

The woman looked up and quickly, expertly tucked the gum in the back of her mouth as she smiled up at her. "Hi, you must be Laura. I'm Jodie."

"Where did you spring from?" Laura asked dryly.

"Tony hired me. He's a friend of my dad's," said Jodie brightly.

Laura felt a sudden rush of annoyance at the idea of Tony hiring anyone without consulting her. After mumbling to Jodie, "Oh did he now?" she headed to her office, via the small kitchen to grab a coffee.

She closed her door and sank down onto her chair. The last thing she wanted to deal with today was a new and rather unusual assistant, hired without her knowledge. She surveyed her desk. There was still some preparation to be done before eleven o'clock and she had little more than an hour. Untimely memories of last night's breakup with Debbie flooded her mind and it was all she could do to stop herself dissolving in a flood of tears.

Within minutes, Tony burst into her office. "Thank Christ you're here," he said. "Where've you been?" He paused then and looked hard at her. "What happened to you? You look like shit!"

"Thanks a lot," Laura said as she lit a cigarette then gulped down more strong coffee. "And who on earth is the bubble-gum baby out front?"

Tony sat down in the other chair beside Laura's desk. Looking uncomfortable, he explained, "Well, I was talking to a mate of mine and I was saying how we needed an assistant, and . . . well, he said his daughter could do that with no problems. Apparently she's had trouble getting a job. So I, well . . . you know . . . what could I say?"

Selecting the right staff was not one of Tony's talents and it had been agreed that she would be the one to make those sorts of choices.

Laura snapped at him, "You could've told him you'd discuss it with your partner. And it's no fucking wonder she's had difficulty finding a job."

The most outstanding thing about Jodie, apart from her expertise at blowing bubbles, was her spiky green-tipped hair. She wore very dark lipstick, almost black, with heavy black eyeliner, exaggerating a ghostly pale face. Laura had glimpsed black leggings under a tight, short red sleeveless stretch dress which matched her red platform shoes.

Tony looked sheepish and mumbled, "Yeah, well, I didn't know she looked like that, did I?" Laura just glared at him. "Can't we just give her a few days? If she's hopeless, we'll get rid of her, okay?"

"Yes, and it'll be my job to fire her, I suppose!" She glanced away from him quickly but knew he would have seen the tears that had sprung to her eyes.

"Do you want to talk about what's wrong, mate?" he asked gently.

She concentrated on her hand as she twisted the gold ring around her finger, trying to maintain her composure. "Debbie and I have separated, and I'm a bit of a mess today. I'll be fine once I've got this work done for the meeting"

"Oh shit, mate, I'm sorry." He stood, looking helpless. "Aah . . . right. Well, I'll leave you to it . . ." He turned to leave. "Oh by the way, have you got the finished artwork back from the typesetters yet?"

Laura remembered with a jolt that it should have

been here first thing. She should have checked on it as soon as she arrived. "God, no. It's not here yet."

"No worries, mate, I'll chase it up," Tony said as he closed the door. Laura mentally kicked herself for not being more meticulous. She was usually very organized, but lately her worries about Debbie had often disrupted her concentration.

Within forty-five minutes, Laura had everything ready. She'd found ten minutes to put on her make-up and perfume, and she felt like she was back in control. She rang Jodie and asked her to organize coffee for the presentation and to expect Mr. Giraldi from Pasta Masta Foods. "Tony will show you how to set everything up," she added, smiling to herself. Then there was a knock at her door. Thank God, Kate's here with the artwork, she thought.

Kate Merlo was a commercial artist who worked for a small typesetting company which serviced the advertising business. She was employed as a typesetter but was often called upon to create whole layouts. Laura had a great deal of regard for Kate's work. She was talented, and Laura always asked for her personally on all Adwork's jobs. It didn't hurt either that she was a dyke and very attractive at that. Laura liked Kate and considered her efficient and friendly. Her interest ended there.

It was an entirely different situation for Kate. Her eyes had locked onto Laura the first time they'd met a year ago, and Kate thought she was absolutely gorgeous. She loved working with Laura and always looked forward to her jobs with Adworks. Her attraction to Laura had increased over time, to the point where she thought about her and fantasized about her constantly. But she lacked the confidence to do anything about it. She also doubted that Laura, whom she considered a sophisticated woman in her thirties, would be at all interested in a twenty-three-year-old.

"Hi Kate," said Laura with her dazzling smile, as she opened the door. "I'm running a bit behind this morning, so we'll have to check through everything quickly. I'm sure it'll be perfect, though, as usual."

She motioned Kate to sit at the desk while they checked the layouts. She stood and leaned close to Kate as Kate pointed out certain details to her. Laura was clearly oblivious to the effect she was having on Kate. Kate was finding it hard to concentrate with her face inches from Laura's breasts. Breathing in her perfume, listening to her voice purring just above her head and watching her manicured hand pointing to things on the page, more than once Kate hesitated when her mouth went dry, and she ached to touch Laura. She kept drifting off and imagining herself kissing the sexy mouth that was so tantalizingly close.

All too soon, Laura was saying, "The work's terrific, Kate, just what I wanted. Thanks again for your input. Those ideas of yours have really made a difference. A great job as usual. I owe you a lunch."

God, let her mean that, thought Kate as Laura opened the door.

* * * * *

Kate paused in the doorway. She combed her long dark hair back from her face with her fingers; a habit Laura liked. She was smiling, clearly pleased that the job had worked out well. Her brown eyes gazed into Laura's with a directness that Laura always found rather disarming.

"Good luck with the presentation," said Kate as she left.

At eleven o'clock, Tony poked his head around her door. "Giraldi's here. I'll start with all the numbers stuff as usual. You come in for your bit in about fifteen minutes, okay?"

Laura nodded. "Good luck, Tony."

"By the way," Tony added, "I can't take him to lunch today. I've had a call from Lachlan about an urgent campaign. I've got to go and see him straight after this meeting. Sorry."

"You can't do this to me, Tony. I don't think I can cope with him on my own today," Laura pleaded.

Tony shrugged helplessly. "Sorry, mate, it can't be helped. You'll be all right," he said with a grin as he headed off to the meeting.

Giraldi was a difficult client, but the presentation was a success. With the combination of Laura's clever press ideas and Tony's creative accounting and fast talking, the account was won. Afterwards, they gave each other a victory hug in Laura's office before she grabbed her wallet and keys and left to take the client to lunch. She hoped that she could cope with lunch as well as she had coped until now. This client was an egotistical, boring man who flirted outrageously with every woman he came in contact with, and Laura just wasn't in the mood to have a fat, sixty-year-old man staring at her cleavage for the next two hours.

She didn't get back until four-thirty. Mario Giraldi had continuously ordered more wine and raved on endlessly about how he'd brilliantly built up his successful business from nothing. She'd limited her drinking as much as she could without offending him but had consumed enough to make her feel rather light-headed.

She heard a familiar *snap* as she entered their foyer and was met by Jodie, chewing madly as she handed Laura her phone messages.

"Thanks, Jodie." I ought to do something about that girl, she thought as she headed back to her office.

Tony was waiting for her with a bottle of champagne. "We're bloody geniuses, mate!" said Tony as he poured the champagne. "You were great in that meeting, especially as you felt pretty shithouse this morning." He handed her a glass.

"Thanks," Laura said with a grin. "You know what it's like once you get started, you go onto auto-pilot. It's just another performance."

After they'd re-lived every glorious moment of the presentation and every amusing detail of the lunch, Tony left to go home. Laura then phoned her close friend, Jude, who had left a message for her.

Jude worked in an office in the city and was still at work. "I heard about what happened with Debbie," she said. "Her friends have spread it around like wildfire. How are you feeling, darl?"

As the day had progressed, the situation with Debbie had been pushed to the back of Laura's mind. Now, just hearing Jude's warm caring voice made Laura's eyes suddenly well with tears. "God, Jude, I don't know exactly how I feel at the moment. I think I'm still in shock. I thought I was well prepared for a confrontation, and ready for it all to end, but I still find what she told me hard to believe. Thanks for ringing me. I was going to call you tonight. I haven't had a chance today."

"Poor baby," said Jude sympathetically. "Let me take you to dinner tonight.

They agreed to meet in an hour, at a popular lesbian-owned bar and café called The Three Sisters.

CHAPTER THREE

Laura arrived at Sisters, as the café was affectionately known, feeling unexpectedly relaxed. Perhaps it was the effect of the alcohol she had consumed that day, but already she was developing a desire to shrug off the past. She wanted to enjoy herself tonight with Jude. Tony's champagne and their success today had brightened her mood.

A number of women were already seated at the tables in the front, where simple but good quality meals were served. Laura made her way past the tables to the bar area at the back. She felt the women's stares and thought they were looking at her because of her business suit. She certainly did stand out among all the checked shirts and jeans.

Jude was already seated at the bar, waiting for her. A few years older than Laura, in her early forties, Jude was a vivacious character with mischievous bright blue eyes. Her brown hair was slightly peppered with gray and she'd become a little chubby over recent years. She had many friends, although Laura knew, since she'd been single for a long time, she harbored a certain loneliness.

She got up to meet Laura, and they embraced warmly. "Here, darl, drink this, you'll feel better," said Jude, handing Laura a dry martini she had already ordered.

Laura laughed as she accepted the glass. "Thanks, but I really don't need this, I've been drinking all day, not to mention last night."

"Well, let's take our drinks down to a table and order something to eat so you don't fall over."

Jude and Laura had been through a lot together. They met fourteen years ago when Jude's lover at the time had worked with Laura. Laura and Alexandra had only been together for a year. The four of them became friends and it was a great shock to them all when, a year or so later, Jude's partner suddenly left her for another woman and moved to Sydney. Laura and Alex were a great support for Jude, and over time they became very close.

Suddenly, years later, Laura's life was shattered. On the morning after their tenth anniversary, Alex was killed in an accident. Laura's other friends were a great comfort to her, but Jude really helped Laura hang onto the threads of her life. For the first two difficult years, before Debbie came along, Laura doubted she would have made it through without Jude's loving, supportive friendship.

Seated comfortably, eating focaccia, Laura unraveled the events of the previous night.

Jude nearly choked on her mouthful of food. "She was screwing her boss? I didn't hear that little detail on the grapevine! I always thought she was an opportunistic little bitch, but I wouldn't have thought even she would sink to that."

"Yeah well, I don't imagine she'll be broadcasting that information too widely," said Laura. She took a drink of iced water. "To tell you the truth, Jude, I'm already feeling like a weight's been lifted off my shoulders."

Jude sat with her elbows on the table contemplating the situation. Her head was tilted slightly and she was tugging gently on her earlobe as she always did when she was thinking. "You know, darl, I'm glad you finally decided to bring things to a head with her. You've been unhappy for months and it really was time you moved on."

Laura nodded. "Yes. I should have done it a year ago, but I lacked the courage, I suppose. But even now, I can't help thinking back to when things were good between us and wishing I could wind back the clock." She lit a cigarette and fidgeted with her gold lighter. "But you're right, it's time I moved on. It'll be strange though living alone again."

Jude's eyes twinkled as she smiled. "You're a free woman now. You can start to enjoy yourself again." It was getting late. Jude stretched and looked at her watch. "I'm going to have to call it a night, darl."

"I'm feeling pretty exhausted, but I think I'll hang around here a little while longer," said Laura. "I want to make sure I don't run into Debbie at home. She'll be moving out her stuff tonight."

They said goodnight, and after Jude had left, Laura moved back down to the bar. She was feeling decidedly mellow, wanting another drink. Settling back on her bar stool, vodka and tonic in hand, she surveyed the room. Being a Friday night, the place was becoming crowded. The music had been turned up and the animated conversation and laughter were creating quite a din.

Lost in her thoughts, Laura jumped slightly when she suddenly felt a hand touch her softly on the shoulder. She turned and looked up at the smiling face of Kelly Johannson.

"I just heard that you and Debbie have split up. Are you okay?" Kelly pulled up another stool and sat beside Laura.

Laura smiled. "News travels fast around this town, doesn't it. I'm okay, thanks."

Kelly grinned. "And you're out cruising the bars already."

Laughing, Laura replied, "Hardly that. I should be going home actually. I've had a big day."

"At least let me buy you another drink before you go," Kelly said in her low purring voice.

Laura hesitated for a moment, looking at Kelly. Kelly's green eyes were compelling and they held her gaze. In a confident gesture, she ran her hand through her short blonde hair. Laura liked the way it looked slightly tousled. Her smile was beguiling.

"Yes?" Kelly asked.

Smiling too, Laura said, "Yes. Why not."

Laura had first met Kelly a couple of years ago at a party. She noticed the tall athletic-looking woman watching her, smiling, for some time, before Kelly took the opportunity to come and introduce herself when Laura was alone. Laura was quite charmed by Kelly's confident, easy manner, and aware of her palpable sex appeal. Kelly overtly flirted with her and suggested they go out together. Laura politely refused, explaining that she was in a relationship with Debbie. But that didn't seem to dampen Kelly's interest, and whenever they bumped into one another around town after that, Kelly continued to flirt with her. She had never seemed at all bothered by Laura's relationship status, and cheekily asked her out on dates.

Since she first met Kelly, others had told her of Kelly's reputation as a philanderer. Never having been in a serious relationship, Kelly was often spoken of disparagingly by some as a "love 'em and leave 'em" type.

As they talked comfortably over the next half hour or so, Laura found herself enjoying Kelly's company and flirtatious attention. She reminded herself that now she was single and, as Jude said, it was time she had some fun.

Feeling the accumulated effects of the day's drinking, and last night's lack of sleep, Laura decided it was time to leave.

"Maybe we could get together for a drink some time again soon, or perhaps dinner," Kelly said.

"That would be nice," Laura said with a smile.

She stood up to leave and suddenly felt slightly dizzy. She stumbled and put her hand to her head.

In an instant Kelly's strong arms were around her, holding her securely. Somewhere inside Laura's hazy mind, she was aware that Kelly's arms around her felt good. Kelly's lips brushed her cheek, and she felt a sensation that she hadn't felt in months — the first stirring of desire. She remained in Kelly's embrace for longer than was necessary before she drew away.

She politely refused Kelly's offer to drive her home and, just managing a dignified exit, hailed a cab and went home.

It was eleven-thirty when Laura entered her darkened apartment. To her great relief there was no sign of Debbie, and a quick look around revealed that Debbie had taken her things. She was gone. Laura glanced across at the still unmade bed that Debbie had slept in last night. Her pillow was crumpled in that particular way, from Debbie hugging it in her sleep.

The memories of better times and the impact of the end of the relationship hit her again. The tears welled and trickled down her cheeks.

She stripped the bed and remade it with clean white cotton damask sheets, then had a long hot shower. She thought that she'd better take things quietly for a couple of weeks. She'd found herself feeling very attracted to Kelly Johannson tonight, and she really ought to get her head together before she thought about dating anyone again. She had a lot of adjustments to make to her life.

She must remember to pick up her car from the office tomorrow, she thought as she climbed into bed. Within minutes, she was fast asleep.

CHAPTER FOUR

It was Wednesday, nearly two weeks since Debbie had left, and Laura was having dinner with her friends Jude, Megan and Vicki, at Sisters café.

"So how are you finding life without Debbie?" asked Megan.

"Well, I'm still getting used to her not being there," said Laura. "It's silly things you notice the most, like the mornings, without the mad scramble getting ready for work, sharing the bathroom and bumping into each other in the kitchen. And I take longer to fall asleep without her in the bed. It feels odd. You get used to things." She looked down at her hands, fidgeting with her ring. "And her perfume. I only thought this morning as I was dressing, that the smell of her perfume has completely disappeared." Laura looked up and smiled. "Silly, isn't it."

"Well I'm glad it's at last all over," said Vicki, "You had your suspicions for a long time, and it was driving you crazy. I can't believe that she was screwing a guy though. It's incredible."

Just then, they were interrupted by the arrival of Kelly Johannson. She'd noticed Laura at the table, as she was heading for the bar to meet her friends.

"Hi," she said to them all, then smiled warmly at Laura. "How are you, Laura? I think it's time I called you about that dinner you promised to have with me."

"Yes, okay," said Laura. "Ring me next week if you like."

"See you later then," said Kelly, sliding her hands into her jeans pockets and casually striding away.

Laura laughed at the surprised expressions on the faces of her friends. "What's the matter with you?" she asked them all.

"Kelly Johannson?" said Jude in an incredulous tone. "You're going out with her?"

"You've gotten over Debbie pretty quickly, I see," said Megan with a grin.

"Well, let's be honest," said Laura firmly, pausing to light Megan's cigarette and one for herself. "Of course I'm hurt about Debbie's behavior, but mostly I feel humiliated. I stopped loving Debbie a long time ago and I'm certainly not going to pretend I'm broken-hearted."

"We all know that, darl," said Jude. "But you

don't want to go out with the likes of Kelly Johannson!"

With a laugh, Laura said, "Well, I think I do as a matter of fact."

"Yeah, why not, Jude," said Vicki. "Laura should get out and about again as a single woman and have some fun. And Kelly's an attractive woman."

"And Kelly's had her eye on you for ages, hasn't she, Laura? I've seen her chatting you up before," said Megan.

Jude tugged on her earlobe, considering their comments. "Laura can do a lot better than Kelly. She's bloody arrogant, and she screws around."

Vicki nodded thoughtfully. "Yeah, and she's attractive." Everyone except Jude burst into laughter.

"Well I know of women who've been really hurt by her, and I don't like her at all," said Jude defensively.

Smiling at Jude's motherly concern for her, Laura said, "Jude, I've agreed to have dinner with the woman, for Christ's sake, not marry her. And just because Kelly apparently avoids serious relationships doesn't make her a bad person. I think she's attractive too and from the few conversations I've had with her, she seems like a lot of fun."

Laura didn't add that as she'd looked into Kelly's eyes earlier, her heart had skipped a beat. When they'd met a week ago, Kelly's behavior made it clear she wanted Laura, and she hadn't disguised her desire tonight as she'd looked candidly into Laura's eyes.

As the conversation turned to other matters, Laura thought that if an uncomplicated fling with

Kelly was in the cards, she wouldn't mind that one bit.

One day the following week, Laura was sitting in her office around nine-thirty in the morning surveying an empty diary. They'd got the new Pasta Masta campaign out last week in a mad rush and things for now under control. Tony was going to be out for most of the day, drumming up new business.

She could spend the day usefully finding an experienced assistant without green hair, she thought, who doesn't chew gum all day long. But, she had to admit that despite the alarming pink bubbles regularly emerging from her mouth, Jodie was doing a good job. She arrived on time each day, and although she lacked experience, she only had to be shown how to do new tasks once. She was still a bit slow on the word processor doing letters and things, but she got them done and she was improving. She'd also proven to be reliable taking messages and looking after things when Laura and Tony were out. As if to reinforce these positive thoughts, there was a knock at her door and, accompanied by a loud bubble-bursting *snap,* Jodie entered holding a cup of coffee.

"I was just making some and I thought you'd like a cup," she said brightly.

"Thanks, Jodie," said Laura in surprise. Okay, she decided as Jodie left the room, she'd give her a go for a bit longer. She'd just talk to her about the gum.

She was wondering whether she could go shopping instead, when she suddenly remembered her promise to take Kate Merlo to lunch. She reached for the phone. Today was the perfect opportunity, if Kate was free.

When Kate hung up the phone, her heart was fluttering as she considered she was about to have the closest thing to a date that she could have dreamed of, with the woman she adored. Laura had asked her if she liked Japanese food, suggesting a restaurant across town. Kate said that sounded great but confessed, feeling conscious of her inexperience, that she'd never tried Japanese food before. In her warm smiling voice, Laura had reassured her that it would be all the better if she hadn't tried it before. It would be an adventure.

Laura paused in her reading of the wine list and looked across the table at Kate. She was studying the menu with great interest. Her hair was braided today, and she had pulled the plait over one shoulder, twirling the end of it in her fingers. She was softly biting her lower lip in concentration.

"Do you have to hurry back to work today?" asked Laura.

Kate looked up at her. "No, it's a quiet day. I've given them the number of the restaurant, so they can call if they need me."

"Good," said Laura with a smile. "We can order

some saki then. You've got to try that. I thought I'd order us both a glass of Chardonnay to start with. Does that sound all right?"

"Yes, fine," said Kate, smiling. She held Laura's gaze with her usual unsettling directness.

Glancing down at the menu in Kate's hand, Laura asked, "Is there anything there that appeals to you?"

"It all sounds great, but I think you'd better order," said Kate with a grin, handing the menu across to Laura.

Laura laughed. "Okay, I'll order a selection of entrees. I think that's the best way to enjoy Japanese food."

Soon the dishes began to arrive. "These little fried dumplings are called Gyoza," Laura explained. "You should mix a tiny bit of that Wasabi paste into the dipping sauce. But be careful with it. It's hot."

"Oh, and California rolls," said Kate enthusiastically, helping herself to some. "I've had these before. I love them."

The flasks of warm saki arrived, and Laura poured some into Kate's tiny cup. "You have to pour mine now," she said. "It's considered either rude or bad luck to pour your own saki. I can't remember which."

Kate laughed. "Okay," she said, filling Laura's cup.

Laura savored a piece of sashimi and looked at Kate. She was obviously enjoying this experience and Laura found herself taking delight in introducing it all to her. They talked about all manner of things as the lunch progressed, and Laura discovered Kate was interesting and good company.

"So, you mentioned you paint in your spare time," said Laura. "What sort of painting do you do?"

"Well, I studied fine art at college, as well as graphic art," Kate said, running her plait through her fingers. "I like working with acrylics on canvas. I paint lots of different subjects, but I'm really getting into landscapes at the moment. My style is surreal, though. I'm more interested in portraying moods and engendering emotions than creating reproductions of things."

"Has any of your work been shown anywhere?" Laura asked.

Kate laughed again. "God, no. That'd be wonderful, but I wouldn't know where to start. The truth is, I don't know really how good they are."

"Well, I know the woman who runs the Women's Art Gallery. She's a friend of a friend," said Laura. "I could give her a ring if you like and see what she has to say. I'm sure she'd want to look at your work. She'd have some advice for you at least."

Kate's eyes widened in delight. "That'd be great. I'd really appreciate that."

Laura smiled. "I'll give you a ring when I've got onto her then."

"I'd really like you to have a look at some of my pictures," said Kate. "I'd value your opinion."

"I'd be delighted to see them, but don't ask me to give you an educated critique." She grinned. "I'm one of those people who only knows what they like, without knowing why."

Glancing at her watch, Laura was surprised to see it was five o'clock. The time had passed very quickly. Calling for the check, Laura settled the bill, and they got up to leave.

Kate seemed slightly unsteady on her feet as she stood. "I feel like I've drunk too much," she said. "It didn't seem like we had that much, though."

Laura laughed. "That'll be the saki. It creeps up on you. I'll drive you home and you can collect your car tomorrow."

"It gives you a nice feeling, saki, doesn't it," said Kate as she settled into the car beside Laura. "I don't feel at all drunk, just sort of floaty."

Laura nodded, smiling, as she started up the car. She glanced across at Kate's profile again and decided she was really very sweet.

Kate rented a two-bedroom apartment with another young woman, on the other side of the Yarra River, which divided the city. It was an area known for its good fresh food market, and enclave of gay cafés and bars. They'd decided on the way home that this was a good opportunity for Laura to have a look at Kate's paintings.

"I think they're wonderful, Kate," said Laura, genuinely impressed. "I particularly like these bush scenes." She turned to Kate. "As I said, I'm no expert in matters of form or technique, but I can clearly see your talent. I'm sure the woman at the gallery will be interested in these."

"Thank you," said Kate, clearly pleased with Laura's response.

They stood in her bedroom where the paintings were hung on the walls and stacked up around the walls. While Laura was concentrating on another picture, she could feel Kate gazing at her.

When Laura turned to say she'd better be going, she was struck by the way Kate was looking at her. Her look was openly sexual, and the afternoon sun edging in through the window was casting a hazy golden light across Kate's face. Her eyes held that disconcerting warm intensity, and her hair glinted in the light. Laura, transfixed, shuddered slightly as Kate brazenly stepped forward and kissed her softly on the mouth.

Kate put her arms around her, and Laura felt a dangerous warmth unfolding inside her. Kate kissed her again passionately, and without thinking, Laura found herself instinctively returning her kiss.

Kate moaned, and Laura came to her senses. She withdrew from Kate quickly. She felt disoriented and mortified. "I'm sorry, Kate, I shouldn't have done that." She headed immediately to the front door.

Kate followed her. "Laura, please don't be angry. Are you in a relationship? Is that what's wrong?"

Laura hesitated in the doorway. Kate's eyes were dark, and the passion in them forced Laura to quickly look away. "No, Kate. But that's not the point. I'm sorry, I have to go."

As Laura drove home, she wondered about her sanity. The kiss with Kate had been inappropriate. She worked with her and their embrace was unprofessional. She blamed herself, being so much older. But her reaction to Kate concerned her more. The kiss she'd returned had sent a current of desire coursing through her body. She hadn't had sex for months. That must be it, Laura decided. She'd just have to make light of it the next time she saw her. She'd handled more embarrassing situations than this. She was left, however, with a lingering memory of Kate's mouth on hers, and the disturbing feeling that there was something about this young woman that fascinated her.

It was Saturday, a few weeks since Debbie had left, and Laura spent the day reorganizing her apartment. With Debbie's things gone, she set about filling the empty spaces and changing things around. She'd been to the market earlier and returned with lots of fresh tall blue Agapanthus and golden lilies, which she'd placed in vases all around. Late in the afternoon, with classical music playing in the background, she relaxed in a bubble bath, a luxury she seldom had time for, and read a book.

She was feeling more settled and enjoying her time alone at home. She realized just how much tension she'd been living with. There'd been a lot that was unsatisfactory about her relationship with Debbie apart from her affairs, and life was now much more relaxed.

Later, she prepared herself a light meal of salad and fruit, and took it out onto the balcony. She sat watching the activities on the beach across the road as the light began to fade. She breathed in the warm evening air and felt quite at peace with the world.

At around eight o'clock, her intercom buzzed. When she answered it, she was surprised to hear Kelly Johannson's voice.

"I was in the neighborhood and thought I'd drop by and see if you were doing anything," said Kelly.

"I wasn't intending to go out tonight, but you're

welcome to come in for a drink if you like." Laura opened the door to her a moment later. "Come in," said Laura, quickly appraising Kelly's appearance. She was dressed in the casual way that suited her well, in jeans, T-shirt and a light jacket. As usual, her hands were in her pockets.

"Hope I haven't turned up at a bad time," said Kelly with a grin. She kissed Laura on the cheek.

"It's not a bad time," said Laura. "But if you want to go out to dinner, I'm afraid I'll have to pass tonight. As you can see," she said with a smile, pulling at her bathrobe, "I wasn't expecting company. Anyway, what would you like to drink?"

"A scotch and soda would be great, thanks." Kelly followed Laura across the room to the kitchen, and Laura could feel Kelly's eyes on her. Kelly slipped off her jacket and hung it on the back of a chair.

"This is a fabulous apartment," said Kelly.

Laura handed Kelly her drink. "Thank you. The water view is wonderful. It's always changing. It's great from the bedroom upstairs. I'll show you later. Let's take our drinks out onto the balcony. It's a beautiful night."

The sun was beginning to set over the water, and there was a gentle warm breeze. They sat talking comfortably for about a half-hour, and all the time, Kelly eyed Laura's exposed thigh. The robe slipped off her shoulder repeatedly and Laura tugged it back into place.

Laura was well aware of the way Kelly was looking at her and she was enjoying it. She decided that if Kelly made a move on her, she'd happily go along with it. She imagined sex with Kelly would be exciting and uncomplicated.

"Another drink?" Laura asked.

"Thanks," said Kelly, handing Laura her glass. Their fingers touched and they both looked into each other's eyes. The sexual tension was powerful. Laura felt a stirring deep inside her and with difficulty withdrew her gaze from Kelly's. Kelly seemed to be nursing a desire for her that was increasing by the minute. As Laura went inside to get the drinks, Kelly got up and followed her.

Kelly walked up behind her and slid her arms around her waist. "I want you, Laura," she whispered.

Laura turned in her arms to face her. She felt a sudden rush of desire, making her feel hot and weak. She looked from Kelly's eyes, darkened with passion, to her inviting mouth. "Kiss me, Kelly."

Kelly's arms tightened around her, and she kissed Laura. Slowly at first, exploring the shape of her lips, tracing them gently with her tongue.

Laura was aching now. She could feel her own increasing wetness as she reached up and placed her hands behind Kelly's head, kissing her hungrily. They kissed deeply and passionately and when Kelly moved one hand around to stroke Laura's hip and thigh, Laura's knees nearly gave way. "Come upstairs with me," she managed to gasp softly.

The sky was streaked richly in deep pink and gold from the setting sun, and upstairs, the bedroom was awash with the soft pink hues. The ceiling fan was turning slowly, and the crickets were singing outside. They were standing beside the bed, and Kelly drew Laura into her arms and kissed her again.

Kelly hadn't wanted anyone this much in a long time, and she fought against the desperate urge to just press Laura down onto the bed and unceremoniously take her, thrusting her fingers into the warmth and wetness she knew was waiting for her. Silently, she told herself to slow down, to savor every moment.

Still kissing Laura's mouth, she reached down and untied her robe. She pulled it open and ran her hands down Laura's trembling body. She wasn't wearing anything under the robe, and Kelly's knees nearly gave way as she ran her fingers across the soft hair above Laura's thighs. She moaned into Laura's mouth as she reached up and slipped the robe off Laura's shoulders. She then lowered Laura to the bed.

Laura seemed deliciously helpless. Kelly was in control, which was just the way she liked it, and that appeared to be fine with Laura. Still fully dressed, she straddled her. She looked at the satin skin of her throat and the line of her shoulders, the small breasts with their hard cherry nipples, and across her firm stomach and hips to the small mound of brown hair. Kelly wanted to kiss every inch of her. She wanted to remove her own clothes and feel Laura against her. But she couldn't stop now to get undressed. She was aching to taste her and to be inside her. She lowered her head and took one of Laura's nipples into her mouth, teasing it with her tongue. Laura writhed, moving her hips.

"Oh, Kelly," she murmured breathlessly. She took

Kelly's hand and guided it down across her stomach, placing it between her thighs.

Kelly gasped as her fingers slid along Laura's incredibly warm wetness. She couldn't ever remember touching a woman who'd been this wet. Kelly's passion became overwhelming as she gently stroked in rhythm with Laura's hips. Kelly entered her.

"Yes," Laura breathed, and she raised her hips taking Kelly inside her more deeply. Kelly could feel Laura's powerful orgasm building as her fingers thrust deeply and rhythmically. Kelly continued to stroke her swollen nipples with her tongue, and in a moment Laura's passion reached its peak.

Kelly was in desperate agony by now, and as the tremors continued to pulse through Laura's body, she lowered herself to Laura's thigh and pumped her hips hard against her.

Slowly, Laura came back to earth, and aware of Kelly's urgent need, she unzipped her jeans, then slid her hand inside, under Kelly's panties, into her wetness. Kelly pressed against Laura's fingers and Laura's stroking took her quickly to a shuddering orgasm. Moaning, she collapsed on top of Laura, gasping for breath.

Laura held Kelly's body tightly while they both recovered.

It wasn't long before Laura felt desire overwhelm her again, and she reached for Kelly. She wanted to look at Kelly's body, to touch her, to explore her. She gently began to pull Kelly's T-shirt off, over her head.

Laura looked admiringly at Kelly's firm full breasts, then drew Kelly down to her to kiss them. This was going to be a long night.

Laura woke early the next morning feeling better than she had in a long time. She looked across at Kelly who was still asleep. Warm embers of lust sparked again as she recalled the details of their night together.

The morning was fresh and cool, and she slid quietly out of bed to go and make coffee. Her robe was lying on the floor where Kelly had dropped it last night.

By the time Laura returned with a tray holding cups of fresh hot coffee, Kelly was awake. "Just what I like first thing in the morning," she said with a sexy smile, "hot coffee and a hot woman."

With lots of comfortable pillows piled up behind them, they sat in bed drinking their coffee, enjoying the view of the sea sparkling in the early-morning sun.

It wasn't long before Kelly reached across and put her hand inside Laura's robe, stroking her breast. "Come here," she demanded in a low husky voice.

"I can't," Laura protested. "I've got too much to do to stay in bed all day, as tempting as it sounds."

She began to get out of bed, but Kelly caught her robe and pulled her down. Before Laura could move away again, Kelly rolled onto her and pinned her arms down.

"You've got time for this, babe," she murmured. "I haven't finished with you yet."

An hour or so later, Laura kissed Kelly good-bye at the door, and Kelly said she would phone soon. They'd agreed that this liaison was going to continue, but on a casual basis. Anything more was out of the question for Kelly, and Laura certainly wasn't interested in any serious involvement. It seemed that this arrangement was going to suit her perfectly. Kelly didn't say when she'd call, but Laura felt sure it would be soon.

Over the next few weeks, Laura and Kelly settled into a lusty routine, with Kelly spending the night at Laura's place once or twice a week. They went out for dinner a couple of times and although they enjoyed each other's company and pleasant conversations, their interest in each other was obviously one-dimensional. They had different friends and led different lives, and were both happy to mainly confine their time together to the bedroom. Laura had begun to think she had it all. Her life was reshaping itself well. She socialized with her friends, business was good, and she had a great sex life. What more could a girl ask for? she thought with satisfaction.

CHAPTER FIVE

Jude and Laura were having coffee together at their favorite outdoor café one Saturday morning. They often met at the market and did their shopping together. Their bags of fresh food and flowers were piled up on the ground around them.

"I can't stay long," said Laura. "I've got my family coming over for lunch today. It's my mother's birthday. I promised Andrew I'd cook Thai food, without realizing I'd be pushed for time."

Jude grinned, tugging at her ear. "Does your mother know Debbie's left?"

Laura rolled her eyes. "Andrew may have told her, I don't know. But I'm prepared for her hideous comments."

"So what else have you been up to? Are you still seeing Kelly? Or have you come to your senses?"

Laura shook her head in exasperation and smiled. "Yes. I'm still seeing Kelly. And our affair suits me down to the ground. It's just what I need right now." She lit a cigarette.

Jude sighed and ran her hands through her hair. "It just seems such a waste to me. You're a really loving person, and spending your time with Kelly seems stupid. You don't seem to have anything much in common with her. It's all just sex by the sound of it."

Laura grinned and nodded. "Yep, it's more or less just sex." She laughed as Jude scowled in disapproval. "Honestly, Jude, Kelly isn't the monster you think she is. The reason you don't like her is because you think she screws around. You're being too judgmental." She shrugged. "Sure, I wouldn't want to find myself falling in love with her. She'd disappear in a puff of smoke." Laura paused and sipped her coffee. "But I'm not in any danger of feeling that way about her. That's why she suits me. I don't want to get involved emotionally with anyone right now. God, my last choice was a disaster. Look at what happened with Debbie!"

"I'm not being judgmental about Kelly, I'm being discriminating," said Jude. "I can't stand Kelly because I think she just uses women. I'm sure there's a woman out there somewhere you could spend some other enjoyable time with, who shares your interests and whose brains aren't located in her pants!"

Laura looked off into the distance. She twisted the ring on her finger. "Well, there is a woman like that who has suddenly shown an interest in me. It's taken me by surprise. She's bright, talented, and it seems we have a lot of interests in common." Laura looked back at Jude, who was gazing at her in astonishment.

"Well," said Jude. "You might as well tell me. What's the bad news?"

"She's twenty-three years old — sixteen years younger than me. That's the bad news."

Jude shook her head in disbelief. "You think that's bad news, for Christ's sake? You're kidding. Who on earth is she?"

They ordered more coffee, and Laura told her about Kate, their lunch together and the scene in Kate's apartment.

Laura drew on her cigarette. "I was amazed at my reaction to her, and I haven't stopped thinking about it. She's probably just infatuated with me — a passing thing. I'm hoping she was just feeling a bit drunk from lunch and that she's forgotten about it by now."

Jude shrugged. "I think you're bloody mad. Kate sounds wonderful, and since you've discovered this attraction for her, why not go along with it?"

Laura smiled. "For Christ's sake, Jude, give me a break. I'm just starting to feel like my life's getting back in some sort of order. I don't want to start anything that could become complicated." She glanced at her watch. "Shit, I've got to go." She stood, hurriedly grabbed her shopping bags and kissed Jude good-bye.

"Have a nice day with Mum," said Jude, grinning.

"Yeah right," said Laura grimly over her shoulder as she hurried away.

"Aunty Laura!" Olivia squealed, charging in as soon as Laura opened the door. Bending to catch her, Laura swept her three-year-old niece into her arms and hugged her. Olivia covered her face with wet kisses and immediately began to pull off Laura's earrings.

"G'day," said her twin brother Andrew, kissing her cheek. "I'll put all this in the kitchen." He strode off holding a box containing wine and a birthday cake. His wife, Jill, greeted her warmly as she lumbered in carrying a huge bag of toys, books and spare emergency clothes for the baby. Olivia squirmed, and when Laura put her down, she immediately raced to the bag her mother had dumped on the floor, dragging out all the contents, scattering them everywhere.

"Things look different," said Laura's mother, casting a sharp eye around the apartment as she strode in.

"Hello, Mum," said Laura, kissing her cheek fleetingly.

Laura's relationship with her mother was at best polite and distant, and at worst strained. She had never accepted Laura's lesbianism, and her attitude toward her relationships was dismissive, refusing to take them seriously. Laura had long grown accustomed to her mother's obvious pride in her brother, who seemed to have lived up to all her expectations. Unlike Laura, he had rewarded her years of "sacrifice" by settling down in a "normal" marriage, producing a beautiful grandchild. When she was much younger, Laura often argued with her mother about the situation, trying to gain her acceptance, but she had long ago given up on her. She'd decided that she really didn't need her mother's approval, and it was easier to take a light-hearted view of her ignorant comments.

Laura joined Andrew, who was in the kitchen opening some wine. "So you haven't told Mum yet that Debbie's left?" he asked.

Laura stirred a pot on the stove. "No, I was hoping you might have mentioned it to save me the trouble."

He handed her a glass of wine, beaming a smile at her — a smile just like Laura's. "You've got to be bloody joking. I'll leave that to you."

Laura grinned at him. "Thanks a lot." She handed him a dish. "Can you take this in for me?"

While Andrew poured the wine and Jill struggled with Olivia, trying to tie on her bib, Laura took the food to the table. She had prepared curry puffs, a hot and sour soup with chicken, a green curry with beef and a seafood noodle dish without spices that Olivia could eat.

"These are yours, sweetie," said Laura, kissing Olivia's forehead as she placed some chili-free curry puffs in front of her.

"This all looks very nice. Thank you, Laura," said Mother.

Laura's mother was tall with piercing blue eyes. Her overly cultured voice was a legacy of an early 'fifties private school education. Laura's father had died many years ago and she hadn't remarried. Today was her sixty-second birthday.

"Mmmm, it's wonderful," said Andrew, helping himself to curry.

"Why isn't Debbie here? Is she coming later?" Mother asked.

Jill and Andrew looked quickly at Laura as she calmly spooned more rice into her bowl. "No, she's not coming later. She's gone, Mum. We've separated."

"Ahh, that's what's changed. Her things aren't here," Mother replied. "That's a shame. I liked Debbie. She was such a nice pretty girl."

Laura and Andrew rolled their eyes at each other.

"Well, never mind," Mother continued. "I suppose you'll find another flatmate to move in soon enough."

Jill put her hand over her mouth to suppress a giggle.

Laura poured more wine for everyone. In a nonchalant tone, she said, "Yeah, I thought I'd put an ad in the paper. 'Woman wanted to share one-bedroom apartment with one bed.' I imagine I'd get quite a few responses."

Her mother turned away and gazed through the French doors, and Laura and her brother exchanged a grin.

"You know," Mother said, still gazing outside, twirling her long string of pearls in her fingers. "I think it might rain this afternoon."

They were all distracted then by Olivia taking a handful of noodles and tossing them on the floor, and the conversation turned to other matters.

It was with relief a few hours later that Laura showed them all out. She enjoyed the company of Andrew and Jill and adored her niece, but an afternoon with both Olivia and her mother was quite exhausting.

It had been four weeks since Laura's lunch with Kate. Laura had continued to think about her attraction for her. She wondered about Kate's feelings. After the kiss, Kate had looked flustered, her face flushed. She hadn't shrugged it off with an amused smile as she might have done. Laura had gone over those moments in her mind several times and finally decided to call her.

Kate sounded breathless and tongue-tied. There was an uncomfortable pause before Laura said, "Sorry I haven't called you earlier. I've been very busy lately. But I've spoken to the woman at the gallery and she said she'd be happy to look at your paintings. I've got her number if you want to call her and make arrangements."

"That's really great, thanks a lot," Kate stammered.

Laura gave her the phone number and was about to say good-bye and hang up.

"Laura...?" Kate said.

"Yes?" Laura waited.

"Laura...I....umm...oh, it doesn't matter," Kate mumbled.

Laura was conscious of Kate's uncomfortable, faltering tone. Her heart sank a little as she realized that their embrace weeks ago had not been forgotten by Kate. She hadn't just drunk too much. "What is it, Kate?"

"I... umm... I want to see, I mean, I want to thank you for that lunch."

Laura laughed, relieved. "Oh that. You're very welcome." Laura then said she had to go and they both said good-bye.

Her flustered words conveyed a great deal to Laura and she was concerned. Kate had revealed much about herself during that lunch. Laura had been pleasantly surprised to discover so much sensitivity and thoughtful intelligence in someone so young. Kate managed to portray strength and vulnerability all at once, which Laura found very attractive. In kissing her so passionately, Kate had revealed a strong attraction to her, and Laura had to admit that whether she liked it or not, she was seriously attracted to Kate. She would just have to try to put Kate out of her mind. After all, she was spending plenty of time with Kelly and surely that would help to put thoughts of Kate into perspective.

The following Saturday, having met Jude again for shopping and coffee, Laura told her about her phone conversation with Kate.

Laura stubbed out her cigarette. "So she wasn't drunk and she hasn't forgotten about it. Her interest in me seems to be more serious than I'd hoped."

"Well it doesn't sound like a silly infatuation

anyway," said Jude. "You're attracted to her, so why don't you go along with it. Have an affair with her, for God's sake, and you can get bloody Kelly out of your life."

Laura sighed. "Because, Jude, there's something special about her. Kate is certainly not a Kelly type, and I'm afraid I could get quite serious about her if I allowed anything to develop. I don't trust myself emotionally at the moment. I'm not ready for anything serious and it wouldn't be casual with Kate... Thank Christ Kelly's around to keep my mind off her." She lit another cigarette. She exhaled, leaning back in her chair. "I'm not getting involved with a twenty-three-year-old."

Jude laughed. "Shit, I'd kill to have a twenty-three-year-old panting after me!"

Laura laughed with her and decided to drop the subject.

CHAPTER SIX

Later that week, Laura was surveying all the work on her desk. It was April, and Tony had taken a week's holiday, hoping to catch the remnants of the warm weather. They had expected a quiet time but it seemed every client suddenly needed a new campaign. Laura had brought in a freelance copywriter to help out, and now she needed help on artwork layouts.

At least Jodie had proven to be an asset. She was a fast learner and reliable. Laura had spoken to her about the bubble gum, asking her to refrain from blowing bubbles while sitting at the reception desk or talking to clients. Jodie's solution to this was to simply hide the gum in her mouth whenever Laura was around. Laura never again actually saw Jodie chewing gum but was beginning to grow accustomed to hearing the pops and snaps whenever she was nearby but out of sight. Laura had relaxed a great deal with Jodie, and could see the funny side of this. Sometimes, she even amused herself by trying to catch Jodie out, approaching her desk very quietly. But Jodie apparently had a sixth sense, and Laura had so far not managed to catch a single bubble in the making. More importantly, all their clients seemed to really like Jodie, which was the main thing as far as Laura was concerned.

Laura rang Jodie at reception and asked her to contact Kate Merlo at the typesetters and make a time to discuss the new briefs. Previously, Laura would have phoned Kate herself, but she felt uneasy now about her and was attempting to make things seem more businesslike between them.

Laura's office door was open when Kate arrived and she stood there for a moment entranced, looking at Laura drawing on her layout pad, talking with a client on the phone, its receiver propped on her shoulder. God, she's gorgeous, Kate thought, aware of that familiar aching tug of desire in her body.

Kate had been away for about ten days, at her mother's beach house. She was due for a vacation and had allowed herself to be convinced by her mother that she needed a break. Kate had not been sleeping or eating well in recent weeks, since her interest in Laura had grown to become a virtual obsession. She took a friend with her, and found herself relaxing and having a good time. She put her feelings for Laura into some sort of perspective, and despite the advice of her friend to give this woman a big miss, Kate had decided to take some control of the situation. She wanted Laura, and she was going to try everything she could to get her. If in the end she failed, she'd have to find a way to deal with that. But she had to try. So she was feeling refreshed and confident when Jodie rang.

Just be *cool,* she told herself silently, *don't be a bumbling idiot.*

Laura put down the phone and looked up at Kate with a dazzling smile that almost undid Kate. Laura said, "You look relaxed. You've obviously had some time off while the rest of us have been slaving away. That's a great tan."

Laura seemed slightly uneasy as Kate approached her with a confident smile. *She senses there's something different about me today,* Kate thought. She didn't take her eyes away from Laura's. Laura explained the various jobs to be done, but she seemed distracted, as if Kate's gaze was having an unsettling effect on her.

"Have I made all this clear, Kate?" She was fidgeting with her ring, twisting it back and forth on her finger.

"It's all quite straightforward," Kate replied. "I'll have some layouts for you within a couple of days. But I do have one question, though."

"Yes?" Laura seemed grateful, as if the tension might ease if they had some discussion.

"Will you have dinner with me tomorrow night?"

Laura looked completely thrown off balance, as if it was the last thing she expected Kate to come out with. Her usual poise left her momentarily. "Oh... ahh... I don't think I can," she stuttered.

"Why not?" Kate asked brazenly. She had nothing to lose.

"Really, Kate, I don't think it would be a good idea. I'm flattered, but there's too great a difference in our ages, and well... it's just not a good idea." Laura was rotating the ring around and around, avoiding Kate's eyes.

Kate was emboldened now, and she was not going to let Laura off the hook. "Did you enjoy lunch with me that day? Did you enjoy being with me then? I think you did, Laura, and I think you liked kissing me too. I don't think you're the sort of woman to kiss anyone who comes on to you, but you did kiss me. Why?"

Laura shook her head. Her tone of voice was casual, as if trying to make light of the incident. "Kate, that was just one of those things. You're obviously very attractive and... well... I don't know why I kissed you."

"Laura, I've been attracted to you since I first met you," said Kate, determined to remain in control. "It increased enormously that day I was with you, and that kiss changed everything for me. I really wanted you then and I can't stop thinking about you. Please have dinner with me."

Laura grimaced. She reached for a cigarette, lit it and inhaled deeply. She looked back at Kate. She appeared hesitant, unsure. She shook her head again. Was she going to change her mind? Kate wondered.

"I guess dinner would be okay. You can tell me what's happening with the gallery. But, Kate," she added firmly, "anything else between us is out of the question. Just dinner, okay?"

Kate felt a thrill of happiness. She had succeeded in getting Laura to go out with her, and she could hardly believe it. They agreed to meet at Laura's apartment the next evening and walk to one of the many restaurants along the beach front, just near Laura's home.

Kate buzzed Laura's intercom promptly at seven-thirty the next evening. Laura looked beautiful, Kate thought. Laura was wearing simple black tailored pants and a matching jacket. The jacket was long and loose, with the sleeves pushed up. Underneath she had a white silk camisole. Laura managed to make this black and white outfit look casual yet elegant at the same time. Kate noticed that she was also wearing her few usual pieces of simple gold jewelry. Utterly sophisticated, Kate thought. She nearly had to pinch herself to believe she was actually going out on a date with this gorgeous woman.

"Come in," said Laura with that smile. "Have a look around. I've just got to grab my wallet from upstairs."

Kate stood in the living room spellbound. The view was wonderful, but more wonderful at that moment was just the fact that she was standing in Laura's apartment. It felt strangely erotic just to be there. She couldn't help imagining herself upstairs in that bed with her. She jumped slightly as Laura returned in a soft delicious cloud of perfume.

"What do you think?" Laura asked.

"Oh it's great. I love the view," Kate replied. "It must be wonderful living here."

Laura agreed, and they headed off for dinner.

They walked a few blocks and chose an Italian bistro. They sat at a table near the window where they could watch people strolling along the palm-tree-lined boulevard.

"Would you prefer white or red wine?" Laura asked.

Kate shrugged and smiled. "I don't mind. You choose."

"Well, I think a light Beaujolais would be nice," said Laura. "And why don't we share a plate of antipasto to start with?"

Kate agreed and Laura gave their order to the waiter.

Kate was smiling brightly. "I've got some great news to tell you. I went to see the woman at the gallery and she likes my pictures. I can hardly believe this, but she wants to hang them in a new exhibition in June."

"That's fabulous, Kate!" Laura said enthusiastically. "I'm not surprised. Your work is very good."

"Well, it's all thanks to you," Kate said. "I really appreciate your help."

Laura laughed. "Oh, I've no doubt something like that would have happened for you soon anyway. But I'm glad to have helped. I'm looking forward to seeing them displayed."

The food and wine arrived. Laura sipped her wine

and looked at Kate. She was selecting a piece of artichoke heart and some frittata from the plate. Her hair was wind-blown from the walk along the beachfront and coupled with the healthy-looking glow in her cheeks, she had a wild look about her. Her lemon-colored, knitted cotton top showed off her tan well.

"So where did you go for your vacation?" Laura asked.

"I went to my mother's beach house on the coast. I love it down there. I took a friend with me and it was very relaxing. I did some sketches that I'm looking forward to working on." Kate combed her fingers through her hair with one hand, as she popped an olive into her mouth. Her eyes were sparkling and she held Laura's gaze.

Their main courses arrived. They were both having salad and veal scallopini with a wine and mushroom sauce.

"It must be great having a beach house at your disposal," said Laura. "Do you get on well with your mother?" She was always fascinated to hear about other people's mothers, to see if they were as weird as her own. "Does she know you're gay?"

"Oh yeah, she knows," said Kate. "We get on really well. She was a bit freaked when I first told her, but we talked about it, and she's fine now."

"You're very fortunate that your mother's that way. Mine's a pain in the arse about it," Laura said with a grin. "But then, I guess, my mother would be a lot older than yours and more old-fashioned in her views." *Jesus Christ!* she thought suddenly, *Kate's mother's probably not much older than me!*

As the meal progressed, Laura again found herself

enchanted with Kate's interesting and animated conversation. Reluctantly, she found herself increasingly attracted to her.

The bistro had become crowded and noisy by the time they'd finished their meal. Laura wanted to get out of there, but she was enjoying herself and wasn't ready to end the evening. She knew it wasn't the wisest thing to do under the circumstances, but she suggested they have coffee at her place.

Laura unlocked the door. "You choose some music, while I make the coffee." She removed her jacket and tossed it over a chair. Kate was looking at her. Laura was conscious that the silk camisole clearly defined her breasts through the soft fabric.

Laura headed into the kitchen, made the coffee and poured them both Frangelico on ice.

"The problem with this lovely stuff is it's very difficult to just have one," said Laura, laughing. They sat on the comfortable chairs opposite each other.

Kate had selected an Anita Baker album and it played in the background.

Laura tried to ignore the sexual tension underscoring everything, and finally, around midnight, Kate rose to leave.

Laura showed her to the door. "Thank you for asking me to have dinner with you, Kate. I've really enjoyed myself. I'm glad you talked me into it."

"I'm so glad you agreed to it," Kate said. "Can we do it again soon?"

Laura was feeling that everything had remained under control quite satisfactorily tonight, so she agreed. "I guess we could, yes."

Suddenly, without warning, Kate stepped forward

and kissed her on the mouth. Laura was unprepared and just stood for a moment, overwhelmed by the sensation of Kate's soft mouth against hers, Kate's breasts against hers. She felt her body's sexual response and started to pull away from Kate. Kate put her arms around her and held her close. Laura felt a hot rush of desire pump through her body, as Kate's lips opened to take in more of her.

Laura, as if in a dream, pushed the front door closed and wrapped her arms around Kate's waist. She now responded fully to Kate's kiss. They kissed more and more passionately. Laura felt herself sinking into a warm vacuum, where all reason vanished. Her mind empty of all other thoughts, she was absorbed by her increasing lust for this desirable woman in her arms.

Kate placed a melting, feather-like kiss on her throat, making Laura softly moan in pleasure. Laura's hands were exploring Kate's waist and hips, wanting to feel her skin. She wanted Kate desperately. They kissed deeply.

Then Kate whispered, "Take me to bed, Laura, please."

Despite the state she was in, alarm bells rang in Laura's head. She came back to earth with a jolt, her body aching and trembling with desire. She gently pulled herself away from Kate and looked at her. Kate was in a bad way; she was flushed and she seemed unsteady, holding onto Laura for support. Her lovely brown eyes were dark with desire.

Laura was suddenly afraid. How could she have let this happen? she thought. She couldn't go to bed with this girl. She wanted her too much. She cared about her too much. She'd get involved with her, Laura fretted, and she's too young... *I can't.* These thoughts were crowding on top of one another in her mind.

With enormous difficulty, she stepped away from Kate and took her hand. She led her over to a chair. "I'm getting a glass of water. Do you want one?" she asked.

Kate just looked at her dumbfounded.

"I can't do it, Kate," Laura said softly. "I can't get involved, and I can't just have a one-night stand with you. I like you too much for that. I'm very sorry." Kate combed her fingers through her hair, and focused on Laura more clearly, as if she were coming back to reality. "It's unforgivable," Laura said, "that I let things go this far, when I wasn't prepared to follow through."

"I don't believe this," said Kate, looking genuinely confused. "You feel the same way I do. You're not in a relationship, so what's the problem?" Kate was floundering. She clearly hadn't counted on Laura having any other problems.

Laura was now regaining her composure. "Yes, it's obvious I feel the same way you do. I can't deny that. But I'm old enough to know that some things are a mistake. I don't want to get involved and if I sleep with you I will be. This is extremely difficult for me too, I assure you."

Kate remained silent, just looking at her. She was trying to hold onto her dignity, but Laura could see the tears welling up in her eyes. Laura felt dreadful. She knew that Kate couldn't understand her reluctance, and that she was very hurt. She wanted to take Kate into her arms and tell her she was sorry. She ached to make love with her.

Instead she steeled herself and said, "I'm sure you'll think I'm an idiot, Kate, but I hope that in the longer term we can still be friends. Right now I have to ask you to go home, and it would be a good idea if we didn't see each other for a while."

Kate clearly wasn't thinking straight. She was grasping at anything helplessly. "But I've got those layouts to show you," she said.

"I'll send a courier to collect them from your office," Laura said calmly.

In a daze, Kate walked to the door. Their eyes met and Laura was transfixed by the intensity in Kate's gaze. She could see the first sign of anger in Kate's eyes and as she closed the door behind her, she was filled with remorse.

Laura sat up for hours thinking about the situation that had just transpired. There had only been one other time in her life when she'd been in the same predicament. That was with Alex around fifteen years ago. Both she and Alex had been about the same age that Kate was now. Alex had been in a relationship that had begun when she was only nineteen, with a woman ten years her senior. At nineteen, Alex was too young to make the serious commitment she'd made with the older woman. But she'd been Alex's first lover and she'd just fallen into the relationship.

Then she met Laura. It was love at first sight for them both but Alex didn't want to hurt the woman she lived with, and Laura didn't want to cause a break-up, so for some months their love had been unrequited and very difficult. One night Alex and Laura had found themselves alone, and they'd kissed, not unlike the situation with Kate. Very soon after, though, Alex left the other woman. Laura and Alex were desperately in love.

This attraction for Kate was the strongest she'd felt for anyone since she lost Alex five years ago. There were similarities between Kate and Alex. Kate reminded her of Alex at around the same age. She had similar long dark hair and eyes, and the same sort of self-confidence, which was unusual for someone so young. This worried Laura. Was she re-living the past? She couldn't be sure of that, but she was sure of one thing. If she continued to see Kate, she could easily fall in love with her. She also knew that Kate was too young for her, and a relationship couldn't last. She didn't want that kind of heartache again. She eventually went to bed resolving to discuss the matter with Jude the next day.

Kate, on the other hand, sat in her car outside Laura's apartment for over an hour. She was at a loss to know what to think. All she could do was allow the tears to flow now that she was alone. After a while, she hardened herself with her increasing anger. Laura was being totally unfair and unreasonable. People couldn't choose who they were attracted to, or fell in love with, could they? How could Laura be so narrow-minded? And why was she concerned about their age difference? What did that matter?

Nothing else mattered, she thought, apart from the way they felt about each other. It was very simple. But she wasn't going to give up just like that. She couldn't give up Laura now.

CHAPTER SEVEN

The next day, Saturday, Laura met Jude at the market. When they were sitting at the café after doing their shopping, Laura told Jude about the events of the night before.

"The poor kid," said Jude when Laura had described their unhappy parting.

"What!" exclaimed Laura. "I know it was hard for her, but she's young. She'll forget about me quickly enough. Especially since I've finished it before it began. What about feeling sorry for me? Just at the moment, I'm having trouble getting her out of my mind. But I know it'd be a big mistake to get involved with her, so I'll have to be strong about this."

Jude said simply, "You're just scared to let go, and you're making excuses."

Laura felt frustrated. She'd been sure that once Jude understood how close she was to falling in love with this woman, sixteen years her junior, she would understand and agree with her reluctance to allow things to go any further. She lit a cigarette.

"Jude, how long do you think a relationship would last with her? I'm thirty-nine years old, for Christ's sake! I don't want to have to deal with a broken heart sometime in the next few years, because she's met someone closer to her age, who shares more of her interests. I'm not prepared to take that kind of risk anymore. It wasn't like this when I met Debbie. I didn't feel like I was putting myself really on the line with her. But this attraction for Kate is so much like the way I felt when I met Alex, and you know how much I was in love with her. I couldn't go through that kind of loss again. And I know it wouldn't last."

Jude smiled, tugging on her ear. "Don't you think you're racing ahead just a bit? What about an affair with her? Maybe it'll develop into something more, maybe not."

Laura drew on her cigarette and shook her head. "I know what you're saying, Jude, but believe me, it would develop into more for me, even if not for her. I feel like for once I'm looking into a crystal ball and I've got the chance to bail out before things get out of control."

Jude shrugged, and sipped her coffee. "So what

are you going to do about it? You're still going to see her at work. That'll make it a bit hard to forget about her, won't it?"

Laura looked down, concentrating on her hands, rotating the ring back and forth on her finger. "Well, I'm going to continue to spend time with Kelly. I'm sure she'll help me to get Kate out of my system." She glanced at Jude.

Jude sighed and looked skeptical. "If you already feel this way about Kate, I think it's too late. The fact that you agreed to go out with her last night, knowing how dangerous your feelings were, proves to me that you can't really resist her." Jude paused, looking at her.

Laura avoided Jude's direct gaze, fiddling with her gold lighter on the table.

"Wasting your time with Kelly," Jude continued, "when a gorgeous woman you really care for wants you, seems crazy. I can understand your reticence with the age thing, but I wouldn't worry about it if I were you. You're imagining problems that might never happen, when you could be having a lot of fun."

This wasn't what Laura wanted to hear. She wanted her closest friend to tell her she was doing the wise thing. It was easy for Jude take it so lightly, she wasn't in this position. What she was suggesting would involve taking big risks and a lot of courage. "Believe me, Jude, it'll all work out okay," she murmured unconvincingly.

* * * * *

Tony rang her the next morning. He had just returned from his week in Sydney and while on vacation, he had procured some new business. He asked Laura to meet him at the office early on Monday morning so they could begin to work out marketing strategies for their two new clients. They would be making presentations the following week. This was good timing as far as Laura was concerned. She'd found that immersing herself in work always seemed to put other problems into perspective. Or at least, they receded comfortably into the background. She wouldn't have much time to think about Kate.

Kelly had spent the night with her on Sunday and the sex was as wonderful as ever. This was followed by a very busy and creative day at the office, and so by Monday night, Laura was feeling better. She'd get over this emotional hitch with Kate quickly — no problem, she decided. Although she couldn't prevent the pervading image of Kate's pained, tear-filled eyes coming into her mind at unexpected times. She hoped that Kate had already begun to forget about her.

The rest of the week seemed to fly by as Laura and Tony worked hard together, creating some great ideas for presentation the following week. By Friday night, Laura was looking forward to relaxing with her friends. She and Jude and a few others met at The Three Sisters for dinner and planned to stay on in the bar later. It got quite crowded on Fridays and

Saturdays, and was often a lot of fun. It was here, later in the evening, amidst a crowd of women, with Melissa Etheridge playing loudly in the background, that Laura bumped into Kelly.

She'd appeared out of the crowd and placed a feather-light kiss on her neck, accompanied by a sexy low growl. Laura felt a rush of lust sweep through her. Kelly stood for a while with her arm around her while they talked and flirted with each other. A few times, they'd kissed briefly.

Kelly was going on to a party and then heading off for the weekend. They made plans to see each other the following week.

Jude had, of course, observed all this and looked away in disgust, but Laura was unconcerned.

Kate had come into the café at around nine. She passed close by Laura's table as she headed toward the bar, but Laura was engrossed in a conversation and didn't notice her. Kate couldn't relax. She kept looking over at Laura. The past week had been extremely difficult for her. She'd thought of a hundred ways to approach Laura and a hundred things to say, but she had no confidence that there was anything she could do. Laura seemed to have made up her mind and she was obviously strong-willed.

Laura was standing near the bar when a tall blonde woman dressed in black leather pants and a red and white striped shirt came over and put her arm around Laura, kissing her.

Shocked, Kate stood there watching this scene

with Laura and the other woman. Who was she? Kate wondered. Laura had told her she wasn't involved with anyone. But maybe now she was?

Kate's fists were clenched and her heart was pounding. She felt like screaming. At last the other woman left. At least Laura wasn't leaving with her, she thought. Maybe she's just a friend fooling around, Kate imagined hopefully. Still, it looked suspiciously like a lot more than that.

She'd thought that a night out would do her good, but she felt desolate and decided to leave. She didn't want to go home, but she couldn't stay there any longer, looking at Laura yet forbidden to speak to her or touch her. She drove around for a while, found a café, had a coffee, and then after a couple of hours, resolved what she would do.

Laura arrived home about eleven thirty. She'd enjoyed the evening but didn't want to spoil it by staying out too late after such a hard week at work. She put on some music. The relaxing strains of Chopin's Piano Concertos sounded good after the thumping disco music at the bar. Then she had a hot shower, preparing for bed. She was just getting a glass of water when her intercom buzzed. Who on earth could that be? she thought as she went to answer it, it couldn't be Kelly.

Her heart skipped a beat when she heard, "It's Kate, Laura. I've got to see you."

Laura felt flustered. She'd just managed to convince herself this week that this problem would go away. She answered gently, "Kate, you know the situation. We agreed to not see each other for a while."

Kate responded firmly, "No, Laura. You said we shouldn't see each other. I didn't agree."

Laura was now feeling anxious. "Please go home, Kate. I'm sorry I can't invite you in. It's for the best, believe me."

But Kate evidently had nothing to lose and everything to gain and was clearly going to hold her ground. "Laura," she said, her voice tight with anger, "if you don't let me in now, I'll stay down here all night pressing this buzzer. I mean it."

Laura could hear that Kate did indeed mean it. She thought half-heartedly that maybe she could talk some sense into Kate. She pressed the button releasing the security door. She then opened her apartment door, waiting for Kate to come up the stairs.

Laura felt a tug at her heart when Kate appeared in the doorway. Her hair was braided, and Laura thought it looked gorgeous like that. Her skin was radiant, and there was a determined fire in her eyes that made Laura feel nervous, yet also made her want to sweep Kate into her arms and kiss her.

Kate looked at her and Laura felt conscious of her state of near undress. She tightened the belt on her silk robe. Laura drew her eyes away from Kate's intense gaze and headed toward the kitchen.

"Would you like a coffee?" she called over her shoulder, trying to hide her nervousness.

"Yes, please." Kate closed the door and followed her in. Laura was rapidly thinking of what to say as she set about filling the espresso machine and placing cups on the dividing bench, when Kate suddenly blurted out, "Who was the woman at the bar?"

Laura nearly dropped the sugar bowl. She realized instantly that Kate had been at Sisters and seen Kelly. "You were at the bar? Why didn't you come and say hello?" This was, of course, an unfair question. Laura would have nearly died if Kate had done that.

"You looked pretty busy to me," Kate said bitterly. "You told me that there wasn't anyone in your life at the moment, and you wanted to keep it that way. Was she just a friend?"

Laura was naturally honest and in any case, she had too much regard for Kate to lie. "No, Kate, Kelly is more than a friend. But I'm not actually involved with her — not emotionally anyway. You know the sort of thing."

But Kate clearly didn't know. "What do you mean?" she asked.

Laura looked at Kate's open, innocent expression. For the first time, her purely sexual liaison with Kelly seemed a bit tacky. She felt oddly ashamed to have to explain it. "Look, Kelly and I are physically attracted to each other, that's all. Neither of us wants a relationship at the moment; we don't have those kind of feelings for each other. It's very casual, no strings... you know."

Kate gaped at her as if she couldn't believe that Laura would rather sleep with a woman she didn't care for than with her. She was silent for a few minutes, struggling, no doubt, with images of Laura and that woman together.

Laura had prepared the coffee and had everything

on a tray on the bench to take into the living room. She squeezed past Kate, who was blocking the opening between the kitchen and the living room.

Kate had been studying the floor and when she looked up, her eyes were filled with tears. Laura couldn't bear it. Instinctively, she put her arms around Kate and held her close.

"I'm so sorry, Kate," she whispered.

"Why can't it be me?" Kate's voice was thick with emotion.

Laura closed her eyes. *Oh God, help me,* she prayed silently. "Because you're too special, Kate," she replied inadequately. "I couldn't be that way with you."

Kate's arms were around her tightly, her face resting on Laura's shoulder. "It's because you think I'm a child. You think I'm not mature enough for you."

Laura was acutely aware of the strength, the softness and the desirability of the woman in her arms, and she said emphatically, "I think you're way too young for me, but I certainly don't think you're a child."

Suddenly Kate kissed her. It was an urgent kiss, and Laura's mind went blank. All she was aware of was an overwhelming, utterly irresistible desire. She was falling helplessly out of control. Her heart was pounding, and the ache in her body was almost painful. Her compassion for Kate had taken her across the line, past the point of no return. Her arms tightened around Kate, and she returned the kiss deeply and passionately. Minutes passed, then Laura gently drew herself away from Kate's hungry mouth.

She looked at Kate for a moment, and without a

word, she took her hand and led her upstairs to the bedroom. Maybe later, Laura thought vaguely, she'd be able to find a way to keep this relationship under control.

Laura drew Kate down onto the bed, lying beside her, leaning up on one elbow. She looked at Kate and traced a finger along her cheek and down her neck. She leaned down and kissed Kate's face all over, sensuously with the lightest delicate touches of her tongue. Kate reached up and slid Laura's robe off her shoulder, revealing one breast.

Kate made a tiny inarticulate sound as she drew her fingers along her shoulder, down to her breast in a feather-light caress. "I don't know what to do."

Laura kissed her, then leaned back a little and smiled. "Oh, I think you do," she said in a low husky voice.

"I really don't know, Laura... I haven't done this before."

Laura was completely taken aback. Kate had never mentioned a past relationship or affair, but Laura had assumed that even at her tender age she would have had some experience. She openly led a lesbian lifestyle and seemed to have many lesbian friends. If it hadn't been Kate there with her, for whom she felt so much, Laura would have gotten up and politely suggested she go and do her experimenting elsewhere.

As it was, Kate's sweetness and vulnerability tore at her heart. She looked into Kate's liquid brown eyes and felt a hot, weakening rush of desire for her. She swallowed the lump in her throat. "You don't have to do anything, baby."

She unbuttoned Kate's shirt and admired Kate's

full, firm breasts. She took one small pink nipple into her mouth and teased it with her tongue, making Kate writhe with pleasure. She then removed Kate's jeans and panties and, slipping off her robe, she lowered herself onto Kate's body, to feel all of her against her skin. Breast to breast, thigh to thigh, their mounds of soft dark hair pressed together.

Their breathing was fast, their hearts pounding and their soft moans were only suppressed by their long slow kisses.

Kate had never felt this way in her life. She could hardly believe these exquisite sensations. Laura removed her lips from Kate's mouth to trace around one erect nipple, circling it with her tongue, then the other, exploring and tasting. With a tiny cry, Kate moved under Laura. She felt a sudden painful rush of desire and her wetness increased.

"Oh, Laura..." she breathed. Laura reached down with one hand and stroked the silky skin on the inside of Kate's thighs. Kate was in agony. She needed Laura's more intimate touch. She couldn't wait any longer. She moved her hips in invitation. Laura planted kisses down across her stomach, tiny electrifying strokes of her tongue. Then her mouth found the silky wet place Kate was aching for her to taste. Kate gasped, arching her hips as Laura's stroking sent her into a fever.

This was a whole new experience for Kate. Her previous unsatisfactory experiences with a man hadn't included this kind of sensual intimacy, and she'd never in all of her fantasies about women, particularly about Laura, ever imagined it could feel like this. She was floating above herself, her whole body seemed to be filled with honey, and only her hips moved slightly in rhythm with Laura's strokes.

When Laura entered her at the same time, Kate suddenly felt her stomach muscles tighten, and her whole being became a concentration of sensuality. A few moments later, she was overtaken by the powerful moment, and her body convulsed in ecstasy.

Kate was trembling, breathless. Laura kissed her face and her closed eyes with such gentleness that it nearly made her cry. Kate reached out her hand to her. "Laura..." It was all she could manage to say, and she looked at Laura in wonder. Laura took her hand and kissed it.

It wasn't long before Kate wanted Laura again. She felt even greater desire, increased by her heightened sensuality. All her earlier hesitancy was gone now, and sitting up, she confidently pressed Laura onto her back. She knew what to do. She kissed Laura's mouth passionately, tasting herself on Laura's lips. She moved her lips and tongue against Laura's mouth in the way she'd felt Laura's mouth on her, between her thighs. It was teasing and erotic, and Laura groaned in sweet lustful agony as she pulled Kate onto her, holding Kate's hips and pressing herself into her.

"I want to make you feel as wonderful as you made me feel," said Kate. "I want to make you happy."

"Oh God, you already have, baby," Laura breathed. She seemed close to orgasm, and she took Kate's hand, placing it where her need was urgent. Kate was entranced with Laura's incredible wetness, and she moved her fingers carefully, learning from Laura's responses how to give her what she wanted. She looked down into Laura's beautiful face. Her eyes were closed, her moist lips parted, her skin flushed and misted with a light dew of perspiration, and Kate experienced in an enlightening moment, a new sense of empowerment from being able to give such pleasure and happiness to her.

Laura saw Kate lower her mouth to her breast. She teased her nipple with her tongue then sucked it firmly. Laura's hips suddenly thrust upwards as she was overtaken by the powerful force of an orgasm that left her shaking and gasping for breath. While the tremors were still pumping through her, she felt Kate's hair brush across her stomach, then the melting warmth of Kate's mouth between her thighs, her tongue sending new currents of pleasure coursing through every inch of her. Laura felt her body dissolve, and her mind was a helpless blur as again she came. This time it was even greater than before. She hadn't felt like this for many years. Not since Alexandra. She lay there trembling as Kate came to her and nestled her face into her neck. She was dimly aware that what she was feeling for Kate was an awful lot like love. She blinked back the tears that threatened to flow, and held Kate tightly against her.

"You taste wonderful," Kate murmured in her ear, her hand already reaching down along Laura's body, exploring, wanting more.

Laura couldn't say anything for a while, and she

lay still just stroking Kate's hair. Soon though, Kate's sensual touching, and the warmth of Kate's body in her arms, had Laura wanting her again. Looking into Kate's eyes, she said with a smile, "And you said you didn't know what to do."

They made love for hours. For a long time it was sensitive as they explored each other, but later it became more passionate, urgent and emotional. Kate was insatiable, and Laura was totally enraptured with her. Eventually, in the early hours, they fell asleep in each other's arms, exhausted and contented.

CHAPTER EIGHT

Laura woke late the next morning. She looked into Kate's peaceful sleeping face, and her body responded instantly to the sensual images that at once filled her mind. She was also aware of an overwhelming sentimentality, and she resisted the urge to lean across and kiss Kate's closed eyes. Carefully, without disturbing her, she moved a thick lock of shining hair back from Kate's face. She'd untied Kate's braided hair during the night, and it was now spread out across the pillow, brushing Laura's shoulder.

As she looked at her, Laura realized just how dangerous her feelings for Kate were. Last night, she'd felt completely out of control. She'd known for weeks that if she allowed things to progress to this point, she'd be in danger of falling in love with Kate. This was everything she'd tried to avoid. Her fears for the future were unchanged, but in spite of them, she felt a glow of happiness.

If I'm sensible, I can prevent this from going too far, she decided, *then neither of us will be hurt.*

Kate stirred but remained asleep. Laura slipped quietly out of bed and had a shower.

When she emerged a short time later, Kate was awake and as soon as she saw Laura, she smiled and extended her arms. "Come here," she demanded seductively.

Laura looked at Kate's beautiful body against the white sheets and couldn't resist her. She dropped her towel on the floor. She lowered herself on top of her and sighed with pleasure as all of her body at once made contact with Kate's skin. Kate's hand immediately moved down to the hair above Laura's thighs, still damp from the shower. Her fingers moved swiftly to the warm, already wet place aching for her touch and were soon gliding inside her.

Laura moaned with pleasure and began kissing Kate's neck, face and mouth. She couldn't get enough of this girl. With one hand she reached down across Kate's firm stomach and found Kate's thighs were apart, waiting for her. She teased and stroked Kate's silky wetness, entered her, then stroked her again. They moved against each other's hands in perfect rhythm, slowly at first, but with increasing urgency until, in a rapturous moment, they came.

Laura collapsed beside Kate, and they lay like this with their hearts pounding in unison and their arms wrapped tightly around each other. Soon Kate was kissing Laura's shoulder with sexy little nibbles and whispering her desire for more. With great difficulty, Laura removed herself from Kate's arms, kissed her, and implored her to stop tempting her.

"Please, darling," Laura said. "I've got to meet my friend Jude at the market this morning. She'll be looking for me in about half an hour."

Kate just looked back at her with her liquid brown eyes, unfocused with desire. "Stay a bit longer, I'm aching for you... please..." she begged.

"Oh God!" Laura groaned, as she felt her desire building again. She got off the bed and picked up her towel from the floor. "Kate, you've got to help me," she said with a smile. "Get out of that bed, put on my robe so I can't look at your gorgeous body anymore, and make us some coffee. I've got to get ready to go." Without waiting for Kate's response, Laura disappeared into the dressing room.

The aroma of fresh coffee was tantalizing. Laura came down the stairs and found Kate in the kitchen pouring coffee and making toast.

"Thanks, just what I need," Laura said, as she accepted the cup of coffee Kate offered.

"You don't mind my making toast, do you?" asked Kate. "I thought you might be hungry."

"Of course not." Laura smiled. "I'd better eat something. Thanks."

As Kate turned away to take out the toast,

Laura's gaze wandered all over her shapely body, showing clearly through Laura's silk robe. She really was lovely, and it was hard to resist putting down the coffee and taking Kate in her arms again.

Impulsively she asked, "Do you want to come with me? You'll have to hurry, though."

"I'd like to," Kate replied, looking disappointed, "but I promised to meet Mum for lunch and go shopping."

Laura finished her coffee and gathered up her wallet and keys. She thought Kate looked a little uneasy, as if unsure where things would go from here. "Are you free tonight?" she asked.

Kate looked up at Laura with an expression of great relief. "Are you kidding?"

Laura gave her a smile. "Well, why don't you come back here at around seven and I'll take you somewhere special for dinner."

Kate wrapped her arms around Laura. "We don't have to go anywhere," she breathed against Laura's neck. "We could stay here all night and just make love. We could make an earlier start than last night."

"That sounds wonderful," Laura said, "but I think it'd be nice to go out to dinner first, don't you?" Then she kissed Kate on the mouth. Kate began to run her hands provocatively down Laura's body, and Laura had to force herself to move out of Kate's embrace. "I've really got to go . . . Jude will be wondering where I am. I'll see you tonight." Laura stroked Kate's face with her fingertips and gave her one last quick kiss before she left.

* * * * *

An hour or so later, Kate was ready to leave Laura's apartment. She locked the door as she'd been asked, and was just about to push the keys under the door when she changed her mind. The keys in her hand felt like more than just keys to a door. They were keys to Laura's life. They gave her a sense of security. A sense of a future with Laura. Giving up the keys would place her back in the tenuous position she was in before last night. She didn't have any dishonest intentions, she told herself as she slipped the keys into her jacket pocket. Feeling them there gave her a connection to Laura, and they were a tangible reminder that everything that had taken place between them was real and not just a dream.

"Well, it's happened," said Laura. Jude waited, looking at her. "Kate just turned up at my place last night and, well, all my resolve just went out the window. I lost control with her."

It was a bright, warm day, and Jude and Laura were sitting at a table in the sunshine, on the sidewalk outside the market café. The street was filled with people shopping, and the outdoor tables were packed with people talking and laughing animatedly. In the background, the market vendors were loudly competing with each other, their rough voices singing out discount prices for their produce, tempting buyers to empty their stalls before they packed up for the weekend.

Laura felt oddly disoriented. Slightly overwhelmed, she was aware of a sense of fulfillment, and happiness. The kind of feelings she always associated with Alex. But her obvious lack of emotional control in this situation with Kate made her uneasy. She'd trained herself over the past five years to give and take, but only so much. She'd managed to keep a tight rein on her heart, as protection, but with Kate she could feel herself breaking free, running wild. She lit a cigarette and gave Jude a wan resigned smile

Jude returned her smile warmly, pulling on her earlobe. "I think it sounds very romantic. So how do you feel about her now?"

Laura looked away and gazed unseeing in the direction of a busker sitting on a wooden fruit box playing a poor rendition of a Bob Dylan song. She twisted the ring around on her finger. After a long pause, she sighed. "I'm scared to death, Jude."

The waiter arrived then and placed before them steaming glasses of café latté.

Jude tried to reassure her. "I can understand why you don't want to rush into anything, Laura, but I don't really know why you're so scared. Maybe Kate is your second chance."

Laura looked up sharply. "What do you mean?"

"I mean that maybe with Kate you could again have the kind of relationship you had with Alex," Jude replied.

Laura shook her head dismissively. "That's impossible," she said firmly. Any comparison with her love for Alexandra was unacceptable for Laura. It was already bad enough that she could see so much in Kate that reminded her of Alex.

"Do you think that perhaps you might feel guilty about falling in love with someone else?" Jude asked sensitively. "I mean, maybe the idea makes you feel like you're being unfaithful to Alex somehow, unfaithful to her memory."

This was something that hadn't entered Laura's head, and the concept made her uncomfortable. She drew on her cigarette and fiddled with the teaspoon on her saucer. She responded in a vague tone, "That'd be ridiculous . . . it's five years since she died."

Jude shrugged. "Well, I think you should go with the flow. And stop bloody seeing Kelly Johannson, for God's sake!" Jude sipped her coffee, then added, "I'd like to meet Kate. She must be quite something to have got to you like this."

Laura sighed and smiled. "She is quite something, I assure you, and we'll all go out together soon. But Jude, you're forgetting about the age thing. She's too young for me. Any relationship is doomed to fail. Can't you see that?"

"I still say that's not an important issue, darl." After a few minutes, Jude asked, "So what are you planning to do?"

Laura sipped her coffee. "Well, I can tell you one thing I'm definitely not going to do," she began emphatically. "I'm not going to allow my life to revolve around Kate. I don't want to find myself wondering all the time where she is and what she's doing. I'm not going to wait desperately for the phone to ring, or any of that stuff." She paused while she considered what she was about to say. "I'm still attracted to Kelly, and I feel comfortable with the freedom of that relationship, such as it is. Kelly and I are a pleasant diversion for each other, and I need that right now."

Jude looked appalled. "Do you really think that screwing Kelly will stop you thinking about Kate?" she asked incredulously.

Laura was amused at her shocked expression. "You don't know Kelly," she said with a grin.

Jude looked away contemptuously. "What about Kate? How do you think she'll feel about that?"

"She knows about Kelly; she saw me with her," Laura replied. "But if I know Kate, she won't ask about her again. Maybe she'll assume I won't see her again ... I don't really know. But quite frankly, Jude, it isn't any of Kate's business, is it?" Laura was having as much trouble convincing herself of all this as she was convincing Jude. But Kelly was a safety net, and she planned to hang onto it.

Jude sighed in resignation. "I hope I'm wrong, Laura, but this sounds like a recipe for disaster. If you don't end up getting hurt by all this, Kate almost certainly will."

Laura came downstairs and went into the kitchen. She took the bottle of champagne out of the freezer that she'd placed there earlier and set it down in an ice bucket next to two crystal flutes, on the low table in the living room. The balcony doors were closed, as the night was becoming cool, but the view of the sea, silvery in the evening light, was breathtakingly clear through the glass doors.

It was nearly seven o'clock, and Laura had just finished dressing for her dinner with Kate. She had chosen a dark teal fitted dress, low-cut with narrow shoulder straps, coming to just above the knee, and black high-heeled shoes. She'd wear a light-weight black jacket over this when she went outside. She'd applied a touch of dark eye shadow as well as her usual mascara and pale pink lipstick. She'd booked a table at an exclusive restaurant. She was well aware that Kate was besotted with her, and she wanted Kate to feel special. She also wanted to find the right time to talk to her about the terms of this affair that they were apparently now engaged in.

She looked out at the sea as she lit a cigarette. She'd been trying to cut down her smoking lately, but her emotional turmoil of recent times had set this back somewhat. She was trembling now and wanted to calm her nerves. She didn't know whether she was trembling about seeing Kate again and holding her, or about explaining things to her.

Just then, the sound of the buzzer interrupted her thoughts. The sight of Kate took Laura's breath away for a moment. Kate had dressed up too, in black pants, and a smart cream jacket with a silky black top underneath. Her lovely thick dark hair was loose and shining, and when Kate combed it back through her fingers, Laura noticed the sparkle of small ear-studs. She smiled at Laura and her brown eyes glowed. She seemed to Laura to look a little different somehow. There was an increased confidence in her demeanor, and she gazed adoringly into Laura's eyes with an intimate sensuality that sent ripples of desire through Laura's body.

"You look beautiful," Laura said.

Without taking her eyes from Laura's, Kate fell into Laura's waiting arms and kissed her passionately. She had no intention of bringing this embrace to an end, so Laura reluctantly eased her from her arms and led her to the sofa. Laura poured the champagne.

"You're very hard to resist, darling," she said, "but there's plenty of time."

Kate looked as if she could hardly believe that Laura was actually her lover.

"I thought we should drink a toast to you before we go to dinner," said Laura, mischievously. "A toast to the consummation of your lesbian womanhood." Kate giggled and they clinked glasses, then sipped the cold Dom Perignon.

Kate said, "I think we should also drink to us. To the beginning of something that I thought would never begin."

Laura felt slightly uncomfortable as she replied, "Well, something has certainly begun, Kate, but I think we should talk about how things should go on from here. So we know where we stand."

"What do you mean?" Kate suddenly looked concerned.

Laura was anxious not to upset Kate, or to disappoint her. She smiled warmly. "Don't look so worried," she said. "It's just that all of a sudden, we're having an affair. As you know, I tried very hard to avoid this happening, because I wanted to avoid the complications. But you're a determined woman, Kate, and in the end I couldn't resist you."

"But I'm not making your life complicated, am I?" asked Kate. "Don't you feel as happy as I do?"

Laura didn't want to spoil the night by going into details that they would never agree on. She knew that Kate wouldn't understand that at thirty-nine, she needed to be more cautious about these matters than someone of only twenty-three. So she simply replied, "I do feel happy, but of course my life is more complicated now. All I'm asking is that you allow me to move along at my own pace. I need to take this slowly, and I want you to try to take things for what they are and not get too carried away. Please don't expect too much of me, Kate."

Kate distractedly pushed back her hair. She looked a bit insecure, as if she was afraid it might all disappear just as quickly as it had begun. "So what do you want to do?" she asked anxiously.

"Well, after tonight, I think we should make an arrangement where we see each other only a certain amount of the time. I don't know . . . maybe twice a week or something like that."

Kate gazed at her with her soft brown eyes, and Laura was reminded of Alex. She glanced away as Kate protested, "But I think about you all the time, Laura, and now things are different. We're lovers now, and I'll die if I don't see you every day."

Laura had to keep her eyes averted while she said as firmly as she could, "Kate, that's too serious for me. Please don't push me on this. You have to agree that you've made great progress with me, and I'm glad that you did, but I have to have control over my own life, and at the moment, this is the way I want it to be." She looked at Kate's disappointed expression and smiled at her warmly. "Let's enjoy tonight together, darling, and tomorrow we'll plan when we get together again, okay?"

"Okay," Kate replied with a brave smile.

Laura put down her glass and moved to the sofa. She stroked Kate's face and leaned forward to kiss her. "We'd better seal the deal with a kiss then." Laura felt the same falling, helpless feeling she always felt when she kissed Kate. Their desire for each other was inflamed as they kissed passionately. After a few minutes Laura drew away from Kate and gazing lustfully at her, she murmured, "I wonder when I'll be able to kiss you without wanting to drag you straight to bed."

"Let's just stay home," Kate said breathlessly.

Laura stood up. "I've booked a table for two at a wonderful restaurant, and we're going to dinner," she said smiling.

The background music was a low-key blues instrumental and the atmosphere in the elegant restaurant was hushed. Their table was set with a starched white cloth and napkins, and silver cutlery. Kate gazed at Laura. She looked stunning in that dress, and her exposed shoulders and arms looked golden and glossy. Her dress allowed a provocative glimpse of her cleavage, and Kate couldn't help glancing down frequently. Her hazel eyes glowed alluringly in the candle-light and just the way Laura held her gaze made Kate tremble.

Handing Kate the wine list, Laura said, "You order the wine this time, darling. I don't mind what it is."

Kate ordered a Chardonnay, and they sipped it, saying very little, gazing with an erotic intensity into each other's eyes.

They had ordered entrees of a veal terrine with pistachios, and a seafood crèpe, followed by chicken with a mushroom mousse, and a rack of lamb baked with honey.

The food was beautiful, but they were too absorbed with each other to manage to eat very much, and not bothering with dessert and coffee, they left early.

When they returned to Laura's apartment, they fell on each other immediately, and were very soon upstairs in bed, making love.

CHAPTER NINE

Late the next morning, they were sitting up in bed nestling against each other, with cups of coffee, while looking out of the windows at flocks of seagulls circling above the beach. Laura felt bright and refreshed, despite the lack of sleep of the last two nights.

"Why don't I ring my friend Jude and we all go and have dim sum?" she suggested. "That is, unless you have something planned."

Kate smiled. "I haven't got any other plans. That sounds great."

"Good," said Laura as she got up from the bed, "I'll ring her now."

Jude was free for lunch, so a couple of hours later, Laura and Kate headed off to collect Jude, on their way to the restaurant. They traveled across town to an area known as Little Saigon. The streets were filled with Vietnamese shops, markets and restaurants.

As usual, the main street was packed with people, and they had to often step out onto the road to get past crowds gathered around the vegetable stalls on the footpath. Some of the restaurants were owned by people of Chinese descent and they chose one of these to have dim sum.

Squeezing past the tables crammed with people, and the trolleys groaning with food, they found a table by the window.

Soon, a woman maneuvered a trolley up to their table and reeled off the names of the many steaming dishes at lightning speed, lifting lids for their inspection. Laura suggested they get one of everything.

"Great idea," said Jude, "except the chicken's feet." She wrinkled her nose. "I don't want to look at chicken's feet."

Laura and Kate laughed, and agreed with this exception, and soon the table was spread with steaming baskets piled one on top of the other, and small dishes of sauces and freshly chopped chili. Jude unstacked the baskets to reveal the assortment of pearly-white steamed dumplings and steamed pork buns. While Jude and Kate began to help themselves, Laura broke open the lotus leaf around a parcel of sticky rice, releasing the delicious aroma in a cloud of intoxicating steam.

"Mmmm, isn't this heaven," said Kate, as she tucked into a light, fluffy sweet-pork bun.

Before the others could respond, a little angelic Chinese face peeped over the side of their table, surprising them. A small boy of around two or three, apparently a child of the owners, was regarding them and what they were eating with great interest.

"Would you like some of this?" Kate asked him.

The child reached down and brought a handful of fries to his mouth. Jude looked over the edge of the table to see what he was holding.

"I think he's wondering why we aren't eating proper Australian food," she said with a grin.

On cue, the boy proudly held up a crumpled McDonald's bag, before he scampered away giggling, sending them all into a fit of laughter.

Laura was pleased to see that Jude and Kate seemed to have taken an instant liking to each other. They became very engrossed at one point in a discussion about art. Jude had some knowledge of the subject and appeared to be very interested in Kate's work.

Laura sipped her tea, watching them, and couldn't help smiling to herself as she observed Jude's animated expression and sparkling eyes. She was obviously flattered and charmed by Kate's genuinely interested questions about her.

When Kate left them to go to the ladies room, Jude looked at Laura with a beaming smile. "She's gorgeous, Laura."

Laura smiled, "Yes, she is."

"And she's head-over-heels in love with you," Jude added.

Laura took a cigarette from her pack, and lit it. "She's infatuated."

Jude shook her head slowly and sighed. "I haven't seen you like this in years. The way you look at her, speak to her..." She paused, tugging gently on her earlobe, looking at Laura. "You're obviously in love with her too, darl."

Laura concentrated on her hands, twisting the ring back and forth on her finger. "I'm in lust with her."

Just as Kate approached the table to rejoin them, Jude said quickly, under her breath, "You're in denial, Laura."

Later that afternoon, back in Laura's apartment, Laura suggested to Kate that they see each other again on Thursday night. She noticed Kate's disappointed expression, but was grateful that she agreed to this without argument. Laura had some work to prepare for the next morning and was with difficulty trying to encourage Kate to go home. They were standing near the door kissing passionately, quite carried away, when they were interrupted by the sharp ring of the phone. Laura's muscles tensed instantly when she heard the caller's voice.

"Hi babe, I've missed you. When am I going to see you?" Kelly purred. Kelly had been a long way from Laura's thoughts.

"Oh... umm... hi," Laura replied nervously. "Look, can I call you back in a few minutes?"

Kelly seemed a bit surprised at Laura's unsettled tone, but answered, "Sure, I'll talk to you later then."

When Laura returned to Kate, her mood had changed somewhat. "Sorry, darling, I'm afraid I'll have to really say good-bye for today. There are things I've got to do."

"Is something wrong?" Kate asked.

Laura managed a reassuring smile. "No, not at all." She gave Kate a last embrace, promising to call her before Thursday.

As the door closed behind Kate, Laura's thoughts turned to Kelly with some anxiety. She realized it wasn't going to be as easy as she had hoped to switch her feelings from one to the other. She was still sure that the best way to protect herself emotionally from Kate was to continue her affair with Kelly, but there was a problem. Her mind was full of Kate. Her body wanted only Kate. So how was this going to work? she wondered. It's just that I hadn't seen Kelly for a while, she decided. Kelly was still the same attractive, sexy woman she was before.

She bustled around the apartment for a while, tidying up, and getting out her notes for the campaign she wanted to start work on for one of Adwork's new clients. All the while, she was putting off returning Kelly's call. After about an hour, she picked up the phone.

"Don't be so stupid," she muttered to herself, as she dialed Kelly's number.

"You took your time," Kelly said. "Did I interrupt something important? Or should I say . . . someone?" Kelly's tone was gently teasing.

"Sorry about that, I just couldn't talk before,"

Laura replied evenly. Before Kelly could ask any more questions, she asked, "So when are we going to get together?"

"Why not tonight, I've missed you."

Laura hesitated. The thought of sleeping with Kelly tonight, after this weekend with Kate, just seemed out of the question. "Oh... umm... tonight's not a good idea," Laura said. "I've got work to finish. How about tomorrow night?"

"Okay, honey," Kelly said. "I'll be there around nine o'clock tomorrow."

"I look forward to it," said Laura, trying to ignore her misgivings.

On Monday, Laura was busy working with Tony on the new campaign. It was for one of the clients Tony had picked up recently in Sydney, Furniture King, which had branches in all states. There was a lot to do to prepare for a presentation next week and as usual, Laura's personal problems always seemed to fall into perspective when she was busy. By the afternoon, she'd convinced herself that she *was* really looking forward to seeing Kelly that night, and she wasn't so obsessed with Kate. She was concentrating hard on a layout when the phone rang.

"Darling, I can't stop thinking about you. I had to hear your voice."

The instant Laura heard Kate's words, her heart began to pound and a wave of desire washed over her. She felt immediately disoriented. Everything else vanished from her mind, except for the image of Kate's liquid eyes and luscious mouth. Her body tingled at the memory of her touch.

"Are you still there?" Kate asked, when Laura didn't reply.

"Uh . . . yes . . . I'm here." Laura's response was barely more than a whisper. "You took me by surprise, as you always seem to do. You took my breath away for a moment."

"Laura, don't be mad with me, but I don't think I can wait till Thursday. I miss you so much."

This was almost too much for Laura. "Please, Kate," she said, her voice husky. "You don't know what you're doing to me." She took a moment to gather her thoughts. "Look, I'll see you in here tomorrow. I need you to look at some layouts that'll have to be typeset quickly — that is, if you let me get them finished," she added with a smile in her voice.

"Are you busy tonight?" Kate asked hopefully.

"Yes, darling, but I'll see you tomorrow, okay?" When Laura hung up the phone, she felt shaken. So much for keeping her feelings for Kate under control, she thought. She only had to hear her voice and she turned to jelly. She wondered how on earth she was going to stop herself thinking about Kate tonight, when Kelly came over.

Just then, Tony knocked and came into her office. She welcomed the diversion as they discussed another presentation for the next day, this time for a retail chain of women's clothing.

"Oh God, I'll have to scramble around and find some glamorous 'frock' to wear, I suppose," Laura grumbled.

"Shit yeah, mate," Tony said. "You'll need to look piss-elegant for this snooty client,"

Just then Laura heard a familiar, and by now almost comforting *pop* outside her half open door. "Yes, Jodie?" she called.

Jodie poked her green spiky hair around the door. "This just arrived for you," she announced as she came in holding a box of cut flowers. Long-stemmed red roses.

"Jesus, they would've cost a few bucks," Tony remarked.

There was no card, but Laura knew they were from Kate. "They came by courier," Jodie said, before returning to her desk. Laura was speechless, and Tony decided it was a good time to leave for the day. Laura sat there at her desk gazing at the beautiful flowers and her eyes began to fill with tears. Everything about Kate's behavior during the little time they'd spent together suggested that Kate was in love with her, or at least thought she was. The flowers were a further indication of that. Laura hoped that Kate would resist actually saying the words. She dreaded the thought of hearing them. It had all become hard enough to keep her feelings under control. She also couldn't bear the thought of Kate being hurt.

She looked at her watch, and realized she'd better finish the work she had in front of her, or she'd be there all night. She had to see Kelly later tonight. A cold shiver ran down her spine as she thought of how Kate would feel if she knew Laura was still seeing Kelly. So far, it hadn't occurred to Kate to ask about her, as Laura had predicted. Laura moved the flowers to a side-table and turned her attention to positioning the headline on her Furniture King press lay-out.

Laura arrived home at around eight o'clock that evening. She placed the roses in a tall cut-glass vase on the dining table, then prepared herself a salad sandwich and had a shower. She'd become used to this routine when Kelly was expected. They always had a drink together and chatted, catching up with each other's news, but basically, they got together for sex, and Laura was usually dressed for the occasion. Previously, she'd looked forward to Kelly's visits, but tonight, Laura hesitated about putting on her robe after finishing in the shower. It suddenly seemed such an overt sexual invitation to be wearing nothing but a robe. But this is what she'd always done before, so why even think about it now?

She decided she needed a drink. She needed to relax. As she was heading to go downstairs, she glanced at the bed. Her throat tightened as she remembered last night, when she was sleeping alone. The sweet scent of Kate's body had been faintly discernible on the sheets, and Laura had nestled her head with a contented sigh into the pillow that still held the fragrance of Kate's hair. With her misgivings about tonight increasing, she realized she had to change the sheets for Kelly. She harbored a pervading sense of guilt. She silently chastised herself for this as she remade the bed. What's the matter with me, she thought, I'm completely free, with no commitments to anyone. I'm just being far too sentimental, she decided. It's Kate's innocence that makes me feel guilty.

Around nine o'clock, the door buzzer sounded just as Laura was finishing a very strong vodka and tonic. She pressed the security door release and opened her apartment door.

Feeling fit and looking forward to seeing Laura, Kelly bounded up the stairs. Laura smiled in greeting, and Kelly felt a rush of lust as her eyes alighted on Laura's. This affair had lasted longer than most for Kelly. Laura was just perfect. She was single, so there were none of the usual clandestine brief meetings that Kelly was used to, and Laura made no emotional demands on her. It was wonderful being able to spend the whole night with her, and best of all, Laura was simply gorgeous. In one movement, as agile as a cat, Kelly stepped in, kicked the door closed and swept Laura into her arms.

"Come here," she demanded, before she covered Laura's mouth with her own in a burning urgent kiss.

It was usually at this point that Laura gave in to the fire between them, but there was something different about her tonight, Kelly thought. The usual heat didn't seem to be there. Laura gently pulled herself away from Kelly.

"Hey, you're in a hurry aren't you?" she asked with a smile.

Kelly grinned back at her. "I'm always in a hurry when I see you, you know that."

"Why don't we have a drink and catch up," Laura suggested. "We haven't seen each other in a week or so."

With that, she moved away and headed for the kitchen.

Kelly's gaze followed Laura's lovely retreating figure. "Okay, I'll have a scotch and soda."

Then she saw the imposing roses on the dining table. These weren't the kind of flowers you buy for yourself. She had been slightly surprised at Laura's relative coolness just a moment ago. Normally Laura's response was as urgent as her own. These flowers, red roses, were almost certainly from another admirer. Kelly wasn't surprised at that; of course a woman like Laura would have plenty of admirers. But perhaps, it suddenly occurred to Kelly, it was more than that. Maybe Laura had another lover. Kelly inwardly shrugged. As long as it doesn't affect us, it doesn't worry me, she thought. Laura had told Kelly she wasn't interested in any serious involvements with anyone, but Kelly was disconcerted, aware of a slight threat to their cozy arrangement.

"So, what have you been up to this week?" Kelly asked as she accepted the drink from Laura.

"I've been very busy at work with some new campaigns." Laura gulped her vodka and tonic. It looks like her second, Kelly noted.

Kelly told her about her weekend away camping with friends near the Murray River, on the New South Wales border, then quietly asked, "So, have you missed me?"

Laura drained her glass, and set about pouring another. "Of course I have."

Kelly noticed that Laura's eyes were averted as she answered. Normally, she would have gazed at Kelly seductively, and perhaps even said, "Come upstairs and I'll show you how much."

There was a disquieting silence between them. Laura lit a cigarette and fiddled with her lighter, turning it around in her hand. Kelly felt she wanted to clear the air and find out what was going on with Laura. "Are you seeing someone else?"

Clearly, this took Laura by surprise. It was as if she'd been hoping Kelly wouldn't notice her unusual behavior. She gulped down half of her drink and visibly relaxed. The alcohol's beginning to work, Kelly thought.

Laura looked at Kelly directly and asked, "What do you mean?"

Kelly smiled. "You're not very good at this, are you," she said quietly.

Laura looked away, and swallowed the remainder of her drink. Kelly got up from her chair, went to Laura and put her arms around her. She gently kissed her neck and her face and stroked her hips through the silk of the robe.

"It's okay, baby. As long as our arrangement can continue, it makes no difference to me. I mean ... after all, you wouldn't do anything silly like fall in love, would you? You and I know better than that." She continued kissing Laura's neck.

"How did you know?"

Kelly laughed softly. "Oh ... the kiss at the door, your hesitation, the roses on the table, but most of all, your 'giveaway eyes,' honey. I've seen a lot of 'giveaway eyes' in my time."

"You're right," said Laura. "I'm not very good at this. I really want you to be here, but I feel strange about it. I think I must have a deep-seated purist streak in me that's making me feel a little hesitant tonight."

"Well, in that case, I'd better take it slowly," said Kelly in her seductive tone, "and see if I can make that purist streak disappear. I suggest we go upstairs and I'll take off your robe, and lay you down comfortably . . ." Kelly brushed her lips against Laura's neck and gently pressed her body into Laura's. "Then I'll kiss you slowly from your head to your feet, very slowly . . ." She sensed Laura finally beginning to respond.

She kissed Kelly's earlobe and whispered, "Yes."

Kelly wanted Laura badly by now but she wanted Laura to be as ready for her as she'd always been, so she didn't want to rush things. She made a few erotic suggestions. "And then, baby, when you really need me, I'll go down . . . and tease you with my tongue . . . taking my time . . . and have you crying out for mercy. Does that all sound like a good start?"

At last Laura turned to face Kelly and kissed her sensuously. "Come upstairs with me," she whispered.

Upstairs, in the soft light from a candle, Laura responded to Kelly with all the fervor and lust of their best times together. Once they had begun, she was sexually experienced enough to be able to block out all other thoughts and focus on the moment. It was later, when they were lying on the disheveled sheets, damp and trembling in each other's arms, and Kelly was falling asleep, that other thoughts began to pervade Laura's mind.

The nights were colder now, and the crickets and other warm-weather insects had ceased their plaintive night-time calls. Laura reached across and blew out the candle on the bedside table. The flicker on the walls and ceiling was replaced with haunting white moonlight. Laura suddenly shivered. She reached down and pulled the quilt up over them. Kelly snuggled into Laura, kissed her shoulder softly and was soon asleep. Laura lay very still, gazing at a slash of moonlight that cut across the ceiling. The apartment was silent, except for Kelly's rhythmic breathing. A cold desolate feeling, like an ominous shadow, slowly crept over Laura. She felt a knot begin to tighten in her stomach. Her body beneath the warm quilt felt chilled. Her heart began to pound, and she was gripped by a feeling of panic. It was years since she'd felt quite like this. Despite the warmth of the woman sleeping beside her, Laura felt utterly alone. As she lay there, her body tense, her mind began to fill with disturbing, fragmented images. She saw Kate's brown eyes filled with tears — "Why can't it be me?" She heard Kate's voice — "Make love with me, Laura..." Then Alex's limp body reappeared in her mind and Laura remembered her lips pressed against icy cold skin — "Alex, don't leave me... don't leave me."

Laura found herself whispering those words aloud in the darkness — *Don't leave me* — as with horror she re-lived that moment when her own life had also seemed to slip away. She wiped at her face, wet with tears, and turning over, away from Kelly, she eventually fell into a restless troubled sleep.

Laura woke at six the next day. She felt tired and headachy, she looked across at Kelly who was still asleep, then slipped quietly out of bed and went downstairs. She made herself some coffee and sat looking out through the French doors at the sea. Only a few cars swept by on the Esplanade below at this early hour. A fine misty rain was falling, and the sky was overcast. The leaden sea swelled in oily slow motion. Laura lit a cigarette and watched the blue-gray smoke curling upwards, as she sipped her strong coffee.

As soon as she'd opened her eyes this morning, her first thoughts were of Kate. She was frustrated and furious with herself. She'd tried everything to prevent Kate from becoming an obsession — except, of course, to stop seeing her altogether. That would be impossible. It was Kate's fault too, she fumed silently. Why couldn't she have just taken no for an answer? She just didn't need this complication in her life. Overwhelmingly, Laura was possessed with the guilt. She was betraying Kate's trust and only getting away with this because Kate was too sweet and too innocent to believe she would still be seeing Kelly. But as much as Laura pondered the situation, she couldn't think of any other solution. The fact was, despite her fears, she loved having Kate in her life. She would just have to work harder at keeping this attraction in perspective. She was Kate's first real lover, and Kate was enjoying it, for all it was worth.

For now. But in due course, Kate would move on, and Laura was determined that when that time came, her life would go on as before, undisturbed.

Thank God for Kelly, Laura thought. Without her she'd be in real trouble. Another thought hovered in the back of her mind, however, that she wasn't willing to examine just then. She had woken on Saturday and Sunday mornings with Kate beside her and felt wonderful. She had woken this morning feeling desolate.

She heard Kelly go into the bathroom and have a shower. She made some more coffee and turned her thoughts to the presentation she had to make today at the office. Soon, Kelly came downstairs ready for work, wearing the change of clothes she had brought with her.

"Good morning, gorgeous." She put her arms around Laura and kissed her.

Laura held her close and returned the kiss. Last night, before Laura's melancholy mood had overtaken her, had been wonderful. Laura hoped that Kelly would forget about her initial reticence. "I've made you some fresh coffee," she said, handing her a cup. "And when am I going to see you again?" she added with a smile.

"Well, I was disappointed that you were already up when I woke," Kelly said seductively, "because I was planning a morning ambush on you."

"Were you now?" Laura teased.

"I mentioned a while ago that I had a two-week vacation planned in Cairns, and I'm leaving tomorrow," said Kelly.

"Oh right," Laura murmured as she remembered this.

Kelly drank some of her coffee. "I'm going to miss you, baby. Although, you probably won't miss me. Your new girlfriend will no doubt keep you busy." She gave a wry smile.

Laura looked away from her quickly, saying evasively, "Oh, I've no doubt that some gorgeous bikini-clad girl will keep you occupied up in Cairns."

Kelly looked down at her feet, plunging her hands into her pockets. "I don't know about that. Maybe you've spoilt me for other women, honey."

Laura was rather surprised to hear these words from her. They suggested a possessiveness that was out of character. She wondered if Kelly regretted her timing — leaving for a vacation when some other woman had just come into Laura's life. She was relieved when Kelly looked up at her with her usual confident grin, ending the uncomfortable moment.

Kelly picked up her cup and swallowed the rest of her coffee. "Well, aren't you going to kiss me good-bye?"

They embraced and kissed and Laura wished her all the best for a good vacation. After Kelly had gone, Laura couldn't help feeling slightly worried. With Kelly away for two weeks, what was she going to do for a safety net?

An hour and a half later, Laura arrived at the office, ready for the presentation. To her dismay, she found that the Furniture King client had arrived early, and was chatting amiably with Jodie. Laura greeted Mr. King and assured him that they would start the meeting shortly. Soon after she entered her office, Jodie came in with some fresh coffee.

It was just what Laura needed. "Oh, you're a godsend, Jodie," said Laura as she gratefully accepted the coffee. "How are you coping with the Furniture King?"

"Oh, he's a bit of a dork, but he's all right. I can handle him," replied Jodie, with a small bubble gum pop. Being a bit distracted, Jodie had forgotten to hide her gum, but today, Laura didn't care. She'd seen how well Jodie dealt with their clients, and Laura was glad she was there to entertain Mr. King.

"You're doing a really good job here, Jodie. I'm pleased with the way things have worked out," Laura said.

"No worries," Jodie replied, with a dismissive shrug. But she looked pleased.

Laura found Tony in a bit of a panic. "That bastard turned up this morning with a stack of changes to his campaign. Including changes in sale dates and product lines, for Christ's sake!" Tony hissed.

"Oh shit," Laura groaned. "All the artwork will be wrong; the presentation will be a waste of time!"

"I hate this fucking client . . . he's a pain in the arse!" Tony whined in a frustrated tone. Tony rarely got upset by these sorts of things, which were commonplace in their business.

Laura sought to console him. "Look, all the design work should go through okay, and that's the hardest part. We can present all that to him and go through the copy changes. I can get the artwork changed by the end of the day and send it over to him for final approval. With any luck, we should still make his press deadlines." She smiled reassuringly at Tony. He relaxed a little.

"Yeah . . . you're right," he said. "Well let's go and have this shit of a meeting then." A hint of his usual good humor had returned. Their partnership worked well because they always supported each other. When one was in a panic, the other was always the cool voice of reason.

Laura felt tired and drained this morning but put on a good show and managed the presentation well. The client approved all the essential elements of the campaign, but the changes meant Laura would have a very busy couple of days. She left Tony to go through all the cost alterations and returned to her office. She had a lot of other work to do without all these amendments as well. She decided to phone Kate, and see if she could come over right away and get started on all this. She hesitated before picking up the phone, feeling guilty again. She silently chastised herself, and taking a deep breath, she picked up the phone and dialed Kate's direct number.

"Hello, Kate Merlo speaking."

Laura instantly melted at the sound of Kate's voice. Any attempt at maintaining a businesslike attitude was useless, and Laura's response was automatic. "It's me, darling," she said softly.

"Oh Laura, I've been thinking about you."

"Thank you for the roses, they're beautiful," said Laura. "You'll see them on Thursday night. I thought I'd cook something and we'd spend the night at home. What do you think?"

"The only thing wrong with that idea is that I have to wait two more nights. I don't know how I can."

Laura imagined Kate's beautiful face and closed her eyes in an attempt to quell the longing that swept over her. It seemed like forever since she'd held her in her arms. She swallowed hard, and regained some composure. "It's not long," she replied. "Anyway, I need you to come in here now if you can, to go over some urgent artwork changes. You can tell me what you want for dinner on Thursday."

"I'll be there in about an hour," Kate said, "but it isn't dinner that interests me."

It took Laura some minutes to collect her thoughts and get back to work after finishing her phone conversation with Kate. She was determined that she was going to behave professionally when Kate came in, and then set about immersing herself in her work.

Less than an hour later, Laura got up from her desk and opened the door to Kate. All her earlier resolve evaporated instantly as she looked at Kate. Neither of them spoke as they looked, mesmerized, into each other's eyes. Laura closed the door and then, pressing her back firmly against the door, she took Kate into her arms and kissed her. She just couldn't help it. Kate seemed to dissolve in Laura's embrace. Kate slipped her hand under Laura's skirt, and as her caress reached higher along Laura's thigh, Laura caught her hand.

"Don't do that," she murmured. She held Kate close; their hearts were pounding.

"Please let me spend tonight with you, Laura," Kate implored, "I can't bear this."

Laura looked into Kate's eyes, and saw the same longing, desire and need that overwhelmingly, she felt herself. "Okay. I think we have to be together tonight," she replied. She gently moved out of Kate's embrace then and said, "Now let's try to be professionals and get some work done. If we don't hurry, we'll both be working all night."

Later, when Kate had left, Laura had to admit to herself that she wanted to spend more time with Kate than she'd planned. It was with a mixture of relief and apprehension that she recalled that Kelly was away for two weeks. For now, she had to push all these thoughts from her mind and get on with her work. She really did want to make it home tonight. By working fast, and delegating much of the work she had to finish that day to freelancers, Laura managed to leave the office in time to stop off at the market on the way home. She was too tired to think about going out for dinner with Kate, and looked forward to relaxing at home with her. She picked up some Asian vegetables, chicken and fresh noodles to make a simple stir-fry.

She arrived home just as Kate arrived, and they carried the shopping bags inside together. Kate chatted away about the artwork she had completed in record time that afternoon for Laura, and Laura was reminded once again how capable and reliable Kate was. It felt so comfortable arriving home together, as if they did it all the time. Normally Laura liked a bit of private time in the evenings. When she lived with Debbie she always avoided conversation with her for an hour or so while she unwound, but tonight, it felt good that Kate was there.

They piled up the groceries on the kitchen bench and then embraced. There was nothing to stop the flow of passion between them. Kate pressed Laura up against the bench and kissing her, again slid her hand under Laura's skirt.

She took her mouth away from Laura's long enough to murmur, "Am I allowed to do this now?" as her fingers crept between Laura's thighs. Laura moaned in response, her panties growing wetter with each stroke.

Laura was in danger of her knees giving way, so she took Kate's hand from under her skirt and began to lead the way upstairs.

A short time later, in the last remnants of thin golden light from the setting sun, their bodies were entwined on the white sheets, their love-making urgent and intense.

Glowing in each other's warmth, they came back downstairs, and while Kate opened a bottle of wine, Laura began to prepare their meal. They found themselves frequently gazing into each other's eyes, and they caressed and kissed at every opportunity.

Kate slid onto a high stool on the other side of the kitchen bench, and Laura began stirring the chicken in the wok. Kate sipped her wine, then asked, "So, you must have been in a relationship at some time. What happened?"

"Well," Laura began, "I was in a relationship just before things began to develop with you. But in a lot of ways, it was more an arrangement than a relationship. I wasn't exactly heartbroken when it ended. The important relationship I had was with Alexandra."

Laura paused to drink some wine, then she added more ingredients to the sizzling wok.

"Why did you break up with her?" asked Kate.

"We didn't break up," Laura replied. "Alex was

killed in an accident." Laura was still surprised at how difficult it was to talk about this, even after all these years. She frowned.

"Oh Laura, I'm so sorry, that's terrible," Kate said softly. "What happened?"

Laura swallowed some more wine, and shook her head. "It's a long story. It's silly, I know, but I still find it difficult."

Kate immediately got off her stool and went to Laura, putting her arms around her. Laura looked into Kate's concerned, liquid brown eyes and was once again achingly reminded of Alex. She couldn't prevent the tears that filled her eyes, and Kate held her close.

"You must have loved her an awful lot," said Kate.

Laura was surprised at her unexpected emotional display; there was something about Kate that always weakened her. She didn't want to let Kate feel shut out, but there was a limit to how far she could go. "I loved her desperately, and sometimes, when I think about how she died so suddenly, it still scares me. You'd think after five years it wouldn't worry me." She blinked away the tears from her eyes, and kissing Kate's cheek, she turned back to the stove.

While Kate put bowls and chopsticks on the table, she asked, "Darling, what do you mean about still feeling scared?"

Laura brought the food to the table, and began serving some to Kate. She shrugged. "It's just that when you lose someone you love so suddenly, well... it's terrifying. Your life's shattered without warning, and . . . it makes you feel insecure I suppose. You become cautious."

Kate nodded thoughtfully. There was silence between them for a while, while Kate absorbed this information. "So what about you?" Laura smiled. "How come a beautiful young woman like you wasn't snapped up long ago?"

Kate combed her hair back from her face with her fingers. "Well, I was crazy about a girl in high school, and we got as far as kissing," said Kate, helping herself to more noodles. "We used to kiss a lot — it drove me mad, but she would never go any further. I never could work out if she was just too scared, or whether she didn't feel the way I did. Anyway, later I tried to get interested in boys. In my first year at art college, I went out for a little while with a guy and had sex with him of course, but all the while, I was desperately attracted to one of my lecturers, a bit obsessed really. A woman of course."

Laura poured them both more wine, "So, you began to get the idea you must be a lesbian," she said with a grin.

Kate laughed. "Yes, I was around twenty, and there was no denying it. Fortunately, I met a group of dykes and I gravitated to them, and the rest is history."

"So, do your friends know now, that you're no longer a dyke-virgin?" Laura teased.

Kate nodded, grinning, "Yes, I had to tell them, I was so proud of you."

Laura gazed at Kate and admired, not for the first time, her openness and generosity. She wasn't actually naive, just totally guileless. Laura began to collect up the empty plates to take into the kitchen.

Kate stood up to help her, and in a serious tone asked, "Laura, it didn't bother you, did it, that you were the first?"

Laura stopped what she was doing and just looked at her. "I mean," Kate continued, "I know it would've been better from your point of view if I'd been experienced. I'd hate for you to feel some terrible responsibility or anything like that."

Laura was speechless. She put down the plates, went to Kate and put her arms around her. She kissed Kate tenderly on the mouth. "It most definitely didn't bother me, baby, and believe me, it couldn't have been better." She shook her head incredulously and smiled. "What an amazing thing for you to think. How could I feel anything but utterly flattered?" Releasing Kate, she added, "Come on, let's clean up this mess, and see if we can find a movie to watch."

When they went upstairs to bed, they made love with a heightened sensitivity for each other. They'd shared more of themselves in their conversation that evening, and Laura felt an even greater tenderness for Kate than she had before. Her sweetness, sincerity and warmth were getting under Laura's skin, into her blood.

For the first time, Kate took all the initiative, and Laura, helplessly, had given up all control, yielding completely to Kate's intensity and passion. Afterwards, Laura lay in Kate's arms, her face moist with a trace of tears, her body still trembling.

Kate kissed Laura's forehead gently. "Laura," she whispered. "I'm in love with you."

Laura closed her eyes against the tears that threatened to overwhelm her, and with difficulty stifled the sobs that rose to her throat. With her heart pounding in a confusion of happiness and trepidation, she replied in a barely audible whisper, "I know, baby, I know."

They spent Thursday night together too, as originally scheduled, and made further plans to spend most of the weekend together. Laura had already arranged to have a dinner party at her place for a group of friends on Friday. She thought seriously about inviting Kate along too. One of the little things Laura disliked about being single was the aftermath of dinner parties. It used to be so nice to sit down after everyone left and share a coffee with someone else discussing the events of the evening, then clean up together before going to bed. It was more fun. But she had to fight her inclination to share everything with Kate. She needed to maintain her independence, and certainly not appear as a couple. Laura was grateful when Friday night arrived. It had been a busy week at work, and spending two nights with Kate, and getting little sleep, had increased her fatigue. Not that she was complaining. She was looking forward to dinner.

CHAPTER TEN

It was a cold and windy night, and heavy rain pelted against Laura's balcony doors. It was warm and cozy inside Laura's apartment, and her friends were all seated at the dining table, in the soft light of a few lamps and candles on the sideboard. Earthy, sensual jazz blues could just be heard, under the lively conversation of the group.

Laura was setting down a platter of bruschetta on the table, while Jude opened a bottle of red wine, when Megan asked, "Are you still seeing Kelly Johannson, Laura?"

Jude sighed loudly, and raised her eyes to heaven.

"Yes... very casually." Laura glanced at Jude and smiled at her predictable reaction to the mention of Kelly's name.

"It's been a few months now hasn't it, since you began seeing her?" asked Sue. "That's quite an innings for Kelly, from what I've heard."

"Well I don't blame you," said Vicki. "I've always thought that Kelly was attractive."

Her partner Megan scowled. "I'd better watch out, I think, you're just Kelly's type!" They all laughed at Megan's feigned concern, as Megan and Vicki were devoted to each other.

Just then Jude dropped her knife onto her plate, and at the sound of the loud clatter, they all turned and looked at her. She was looking rather tight-lipped and sullen.

"What's the matter, Jude?" asked Kaye.

There was a moment's silence, then Laura answered for her, "Jude's shitty with me about this whole Kelly thing, that's all. She thinks I'm doing the wrong thing."

"Why, Jude? What's the problem?" asked Vicki.

Jude remained silent and looked at Laura, obviously expecting her to tell the whole story.

Laura sighed in resignation. "Well, apart from Jude's unreasonable contempt for Kelly," she said with a glare at Jude, "there's another side to the story." Laura was suddenly relieved that she hadn't invited Kate tonight. She was rather glad of the opportunity to get her friends' opinions about the situation with Kate. She was sure they'd agree with her decision to keep a tight rein on things. While the rest of them crunched into their tomato and basil bruschetta, Laura told them about Kate.

They listened attentively, then Kaye asked, "I'm confused. How does Kelly fit into all of this?"

"Well, I'm still seeing her because I don't want to get too involved with Kate," Laura answered as casually as she could.

"Jesus! You must be exhausted!" Sue exclaimed.

This was followed by a loud groan from Jude and giggles from the others. Laura then got up from the table and went into the kitchen to add cream to the mushroom sauce. Being open-plan, the living and dining areas were in Laura's full view, and while she stirred the sauce, the conversation continued.

"You should see them together for Christ's sake," said Jude. "They look like they're both madly in love to me."

Laura snapped, "Oh come on, Jude, you're making a lot of assumptions here."

"Okay, you tell me that Kate isn't in love with you," she challenged. Laura looked away, and declined to answer.

Megan seemed puzzled. "Why are you trying to stop yourself becoming involved with her, Laura?"

Laura gave the other sauce, Amatriciana, a final stir and tasted it for chili. Satisfied, she began spooning it over a big plate of steaming fettuccine. Vicki was on the other side of the bench, cutting up crusty bread. "Because, Megan, she's so young, and because I'm her first real lover, and because it wouldn't have a hope of lasting. If I let things develop, there'd be no half measures for me with Kate, and I don't want to invest my heart and soul in a relationship that I believe is doomed to fail."

Jude shook her head, looking at Megan. "Couldn't you just kill her?" she murmured, as she got up to open another bottle of wine.

Laura spooned the creamy mushroom sauce over the tortellini, and took both plates of pasta to the table, to squeals of delight from her guests. Sue had been tossing the salad in the kitchen and now placed it in the center of the table.

Everyone began serving themselves, then Sue asked, "How young is she?"

"She's only twenty-three," Laura replied.

"Shit!" exclaimed Megan.

"So you can see why I'm being so cautious," said Laura.

"No, not necessarily, it depends what she's like," suggested Vicki.

Laura smiled. "She's utterly gorgeous. She's very bright, and she paints pictures in her spare time. I have to admit that I'm constantly surprised at how much we have in common given the difference in our ages." She paused and held her glass out to Jude for more wine. "She seems mature for her age."

"Christ, what's wrong with her then?" asked Kaye.

Laura ate some pasta, which was growing cold on her plate, then grinned at Kaye. I just think she's too young to make a serious long-term commitment to anyone. And I'm not prepared to get involved with someone who I believe won't be staying around."

"That makes sense," said Sue, nodding in agreement.

"I don't know about that, sweetheart," said Kaye. "When we got together six years ago, we didn't know if it would last. Who ever knows that?"

Megan had been watching Laura thoughtfully. She had been Laura's friend for over ten years. "There's something I think I've missed here, Laura. You've made your reservations quite clear, and they sound logical enough," she said, "but I'm wondering how you actually *feel* about her."

Laura looked at her hands, rotating the ring on her finger. "Megan, if I'm not very careful, I'll fall hopelessly in love with her. I'm just managing to keep some control of myself. But it's terribly difficult. When I don't see her, I miss her dreadfully, and when I'm with her, it's a constant battle to keep myself together." Laura paused and everyone was quiet, waiting for her to continue. She lit a cigarette and inhaled deeply. "After less than a week, after spending only three nights with her, she's told me she's in love with me. It's all just running away from me. It's all too fast and it's all too much." Laura picked up her glass and drank deeply.

Megan asked gently, "How long did it take you to fall in love with Alex?"

Laura glanced away, murmuring, "That was different."

Jude topped up Laura's glass. "Don't forget, darl, Kate's been seriously attracted to you for a long time. It's not a sudden thing for her. It's obviously not a mere infatuation."

Sue asked, "So you're the first woman she's ever had sex with, did you say?"

Kaye giggled. "So is she a fast learner?"

Laura smiled, and her cheeks colored slightly. "Oh

yes, very fast." She got up from the table then, and began to clear the plates for dessert.

Jude helped her carry them out to the kitchen. She gave Laura a hug. "I've said this before, Laura, but I reckon you're already in love with her, and you should stop fighting it."

Laura returned to the table with the cake, while Sue and Kaye put out plates and coffee cups.

Sue said, "Well, I think Laura's being very sensible. This Kate sounds very nice and everything, but at only twenty-three, she's a bit young to be sure of what she wants. Laura could end up in a terrible mess."

Jude intervened from the kitchen where she was grinding beans. "For Christ's sake, Sue! Laura was only twenty-three when she fell in love with Alex, and I have no doubt that if Alex hadn't died, she'd still be in love with her."

Vicki said, "Laura, it seems to me that you've been going to an awful lot of trouble to protect yourself from being hurt, but isn't it hurting you now, holding back like this? Why not let go?"

Kaye had just got up and changed the music. K.D. Lang's "Constant Craving" began to fill the room. Kaye's eyes were sparkling with amusement. "What's this?" Laura asked her with irony, "you're setting my life to music now?"

Everyone laughed. Laura went to the sideboard to put out the brandy and liqueurs, and Jude brought in the coffee.

Responding to Vicki's comment, Laura said, "Years ago, I would have said the same thing you're saying now. But I feel different since Alex died. I can't help believing that I'd lose Kate too, or anyone else for that matter." She looked around at the faces of her friends and added, "I know it sounds stupid, but one day, life seems perfect, then the next day, it's suddenly all over. It just seems easier to avoid it all. I never expected to love anyone again the way I loved Alex." She suddenly felt tears pricking at her eyes.

"It's not stupid at all, Laura." said Megan warmly, "We all remember very well what you went through."

Jude said, "I think there's a part of you that feels guilty about loving another woman besides Alex." Laura spooned sugar into her coffee, and stirred it slowly.

"She'd want you to find that kind of love again. She'd want you to be happy," Megan said.

Laura concentrated on her coffee cup as she fought to retain control of her emotions. She knew there was a lot of truth in her friends' words. She'd wrapped her heart in the nurturing, precious memory of Alex and buried it when she buried her. For the past five years she'd kept this love alive as a separate part of herself that, so far, had remained undisturbed. To give herself up to Kate — give her heart to her — not only exposed her again to all the inherent risks, it also felt like the ultimate betrayal of Alex.

Sue asked, "Does seeing Kelly really help you keep an emotional distance from Kate?"

Laura sipped her cognac. "To some degree. But increasingly, I'm feeling guilty about seeing her, and I'm terrified of Kate knowing."

"Well, you know what to do about that," said

Jude vehemently. "Get rid of the bitch!" Everyone, including Laura, laughed at Jude's furious expression, emphasized by her fist thumping the table.

The conversation and laughter continued, and since it was Friday, they all settled in for a long night. It was around two o'clock when they finally left. When Laura climbed the stairs to bed, she thought of Kate, wondered if she was asleep, and couldn't help wishing she was here with her.

CHAPTER ELEVEN

The next day Kate arrived at Laura's apartment to spend the weekend together as planned. Because Kate shared her apartment with someone, they always preferred the privacy at Laura's place. They spent a relaxing weekend together, reading, talking, cooking and making love.

Over the next week, they spent most of their time together, with Kate staying at Laura's apartment far more frequently than Laura had planned. Her distraction, her protection, Kelly, was still in Cairns.

On Thursday night, after dinner, when they were

seated comfortably in the living room, their conversation turned to vacation stories. Kate suddenly had an idea.

"Laura, why don't we go away for a weekend, maybe this coming weekend," she suggested excitedly.

Over the last five days, Laura had given some consideration to the encouraging comments of her friends, but she'd grown increasingly concerned about how cozy everything had become with Kate. Without Kelly around, it was very difficult to find a reason not to be with Kate. The one night she had insisted they be apart, she'd missed Kate and spent the night thinking about her anyway. Now, a weekend away together?

Then she thought, why not. Laura replied with a smile, "Where would you like to go?"

"We could go to my Mum's beach house if she's not using it. It's a great house — I've love you to see it. It has open fires and it's right on the beach — you can hear the waves crashing at night . . ." Kate's voice trailed off.

Frowning, Laura got up from the sofa and walked across to the French doors, staring out into the darkness.

Kate was looking at Laura. "Laura, what's wrong?"

With an effort, Laura turned to her, trying to appear calm. "Nothing's wrong, I just don't like beach holidays, that's all," she replied evasively.

Kate smiled. "Everyone likes the beach. It's beautiful there, walking along the sand with the sun setting and everything. Besides, you live here, opposite a beach."

"Oh, that's completely different. This is the edge

of the bay. The water's calm, and paths are built all around the edges. There's nothing wild about it. You're talking about the ocean. I'd really rather go up into the country somewhere, Kate."

She walked back to her seat beside Kate on the sofa. Laura put her arms around Kate and kissed her. "Let's go up to Daylesford and stay in a guesthouse. It'll be beautiful there now that autumn's beginning."

Kate agreed it sounded wonderful, so they made their plans for the weekend.

Early on Saturday morning, they set off for the small country town, about an hour and a half northwest of Melbourne. It was set in beautiful rolling hills, and famous for its mineral springs. With a large population of gays and lesbians, there were plenty of gay guesthouses and hotels. They selected one of these, and spent the day walking in the nearby forest and enjoying a traditional afternoon tea in town. Later that night, after dinner, when they were in their room, replete with big brass bed, warm crackling fire and glasses of red wine, Kate asked Laura about her peculiar reaction to the idea of them staying at the beach.

"It's just that you acted so strangely, and looked upset about it," said Kate.

Laura hesitated, and poured them both some more wine. "Well, it's stupid really. I should've found a way to deal with it by now." Kate was silent as Laura tossed some more wood on the fire and they watched the rising shower of red sparks disappear up the chimney. Laura was kneeling on the floor in front of the fire, and Kate was sitting on the edge of the bed. Laura continued, "I used to love the ocean. The roughness and the wildness of it. But it lost its attraction for me; I don't see the beauty in it anymore." Laura paused thoughtfully, and sipped her wine. "Sometimes, when it's stormy at home, and the water gets rough, I can't stand looking at it." Laura took a deep breath. "I lost Alex to the sea. She drowned."

Kate instantly went to her and put her arms around her. "Oh darling, I'm sorry," she said. "I would never have suggested it if I'd known."

Laura looked into Kate's warm, compassionate eyes, and smiled at her. "I know that, but you couldn't have known. I should have told you before."

"I don't want you to get upset. You don't have to tell me about it if you'd rather not."

"I want to tell you." Laura gently stroked Kate's cheek, thinking again how sweet she was.

"About two years before Alex died, we'd finally saved up enough money to buy a small beach cottage ... we put down a deposit, anyway. We were paying off a house in Melbourne too, so it was really stretching us financially. It was only a little shack, really. The paint was all peeling, and we put in a lot of work fixing it up. But the best thing was that it was right on the beach. It was built into the side of a cliff, and there were steps cut into the rock leading down to the beach. It was very private there. There weren't many other houses close by, and the beach was very rocky, and the water was rough around the cliffs. It was the back beach, some distance from the calmer sandy beach where the families and holiday-makers went. Some brave surfers used to come there. Anyway, the expense was worth it; we spent nearly every weekend there, often with friends staying with us. I really enjoyed the beach, but Alex just loved it. She was a really good swimmer; it was hard to get her out of the water. She'd swim in all conditions, when it was far too cold for me. She liked surfing too, which used to scare me sometimes."

Laura paused and drained her glass. Kate refilled it for her, and kissed her cheek. "We'd taken a week's vacation — it was late summer. We were there celebrating our tenth anniversary. We'd been there for four days, and the weather had been perfect. Our anniversary was on the Saturday, and in the morning, after an early swim, we bought a fresh crayfish, straight off a fishing boat down at the docks." Laura paused for a moment as her mind filled with the memories. She smiled. "We had a romantic dinner with champagne and talked about all the crazy things we'd done together over the years. We adored each other; things only seemed to get better."

Laura got up then, and taking the fire poker, she turned the blackened logs, causing the flames to leap to life, burning brightly. It was very quiet in their room, apart from the crackling of the fire, and the ticking of an old clock on the mantel.

"It had suddenly grown cold that evening, and we'd lit a fire. After dinner, we made love on the floor in front of the hearth. I remember hearing the wind howling outside as a storm blew up." Laura laughed softly. "I remember Alex teasing me, because I insisted on getting a blanket from our bed to put over the rug. I thought the rug might be dirty from the fireplace. The next morning, Alex wanted to get up early, to go for a swim before breakfast, but I wouldn't let her. I wanted to make love to her again and dragged her back into bed. Of course, I could see later that I should have let her go."

She went over to the window and looked out at the huge full moon and the carpet of stars in the clear country sky. Gazing out of the window, her back to Kate, she continued, "Later, after breakfast, we went down to the beach together. We walked along the sand for a while, looking in the rock pools. The tide had gone out. Alex decided she wanted to go for a swim. She tried to talk me into going with her, but it was too cold, so I sat down on the wet sand and watched her wade out into the water. She had to go a long way out before it was deep enough to swim. When the water was around her waist, she turned and waved at me. She seemed so far away. Then she turned away and dived under."

Laura was finding it increasingly difficult to retain her composure, and she paused, running her hand agitatedly across her brow.

"She just disappeared. I waited to see her come up again, but she didn't. I just couldn't believe it. She just disappeared. I never saw her alive again." The tears overwhelmed her now, and were coursing down her face. She sank down into a chair beside the window.

Kate rushed to her and held her close. "I'm so sorry, Laura," Kate said softly, her voice thick with emotion. "I wish she hadn't died."

Laura saw Kate's face was also wet with tears. Laura held her tightly, and rested her head against her breasts. With difficulty, Laura went on. "I waited for a few minutes for her to resurface. The water was very rough out there, and it was infamous for the dangerous current that pulled the water around the cliff. I started yelling out to her. I ran out into the water until I was chest deep, but I couldn't see her. The waves were starting to get bigger as the tide began to come in. It turned out that I was there for about half an hour, getting knocked over by the waves and screaming. Some people in a boat some distance away saw me, and they came closer to find out what was wrong. It was risky bringing a boat that far in. Anyway, they dragged me onto the boat, and we headed around to the other side of the cliff. The guy said she must have been caught in the rip, so we should go with the current to find her. He was right. We found her washed up on the rocks a couple of kilometers away. We couldn't get anywhere near her because of the rocks, so he got on the radio to the coast guard. I was hysterical. I could see her lying there with the waves washing over her, and I couldn't get near her. I was out of my mind, and I tried to jump out of the boat and swim to her — as if I could. It took both the guy and the woman with him, to hold me back and calm me. I was just praying that she was alive."

Laura released herself from Kate's arms and walked over to the fire. She suddenly felt cold. Kate handed her a tissue and she dried her tears.

"The people on the boat took me back to the beach, and I ran all the way around the cliffs, through the scrub, to get to the place where she was lying. She was a long way down, and it was impossible for me to climb down anyway. The rescue people went down on ropes, and they brought her up in a harness. She wasn't injured . . . she'd drowned before she was washed up on the rocks. I can't remember everything that happened after that. But I can remember begging her to wake up. She was ice cold. I was holding her tightly, and I remember the incredible weight of her. I was kissing her, my mouth covered in sand, she was salty. I began to shake her, pleading with her not to die, not to leave me."

Laura put her face in her hands, as she was suddenly swamped with grief. She took a deep breath and gazed into the leaping flames. "They had to drag me off her and restrain me, so they could put her into the ambulance. They treated me for shock and gave me something which knocked me out for a few hours. I stayed in hospital overnight. For a long time, I wished I'd died with her."

Laura turned then and looked at Kate, who was sobbing. Kate came to her, and held her tightly.

"Oh Laura, I'm so sorry. I can't bear to think what you went through." She kissed Laura's face, her eyes, and her lips. Kate broke down in a flood of tears.

Laura kissed her. "Look how upset I've made you," she said. "I'm sorry, baby. Don't cry anymore, it's over now." She wondered, as she kissed Kate's wet face, soothing her, whether it would ever really be over for her.

A short time later, they were cuddled up together in the cozy bed. The fire was burning brightly in the grate, casting warm comforting flickering patterns on the walls. Kate held Laura close and stroked her hair, and soon Laura was fast asleep. Kate lay awake for a long time. Suddenly a lot of things made sense to her. She understood now why Laura was so reluctant to allow a relationship to develop between them. No wonder she was scared. Kate's heart was bursting with love for Laura and as she held her in her arms, she decided that she would be patient. I have to make her really see how much I love her, Kate thought, let her see that she can trust me. She resolved to accept Laura's conditions that they not see each other too much, without giving Laura a hard time about it. Kate then snuggled in against Laura's warm body and decided it wouldn't be long before she and Laura would be together, properly, forever. With a contented sigh, Kate fell asleep.

They returned to Melbourne late on Sunday afternoon, and it was decided that Kate would spend the night again with Laura. Kate decided she wanted to cook dinner for Laura, and they stopped off at the supermarket on the way home.

She cooked roast lamb with mint sauce and baked vegetables. It was good to see Laura on the other side of the kitchen bench for a change, relaxing with a glass of wine while Kate did the cooking. Laura seemed to enjoy it immensely.

Over Amaretto and coffee, Laura suggested they should slow things down a bit in the coming week. "What about your friends, and all the other things you like to do?"

Kate, remembering her private pledge to be patient, bit her lip, and nodded in acquiescence.

CHAPTER TWELVE

During the busy afternoon on Wednesday, Laura was working at her desk, when her phone rang. She expected it would be Kate. They'd spoken on the phone each day, but they hadn't seen each other since Monday morning, when they both left Laura's apartment for work. Laura was looking forward to seeing Kate tonight.

Laura was completely taken aback to hear Kelly's voice. She quickly collected her thoughts. "Oh, Kelly, umm... how was Cairns?" Laura replied.

"It was great. I thought maybe you'd like to see

my all-over tan," said Kelly in her low seductive voice. "Maybe on Friday night?"

Laura's mind worked rapidly. It wasn't all that long ago that a conversation like this with Kelly would have had her heart pounding with lustful anticipation. Now it was pounding with anxiety.

After a brief pause, Laura replied warmly, "Okay, Friday will be fine."

That night with Kate, Laura felt decidedly uneasy. When Kate suggested that they get together on Friday night and spend the weekend together, Laura had to avert her eyes. She'd already told Kate she wasn't free on Friday night. Without argument, Kate agreed to come around late on Saturday afternoon. Every time Laura looked into Kate's eyes or held her and kissed her, she secretly resolved to ring Kelly and cancel their arrangement. But over and over she silently told herself this was the only way to keep herself in check. Later that night, when Kate was lying hot and naked in her arms, her breathing fast and shallow, her eyes worshipful, Laura felt her heart melt and she made love to Kate with more passion and tenderness than ever before. Laura couldn't be satisfied enough that night. She couldn't have enough of Kate. She couldn't let her go.

"Vodka and tonic?" Tony asked Laura. It had been rather quiet for a Friday, and Laura lingered unnecessarily in the office.

"Yeah, a strong one please," said Laura, as she sank into a comfortable leather chair in Tony's office. She was in no hurry to go home; she wasn't looking forward to tonight. She was quite happy about the idea of seeing Kelly and talking with her. Kelly could be very amusing, and she was sure Kelly would have some funny stories about her vacation. And she still found Kelly very attractive. But her feelings for Kate and her guilt were rapidly dousing the flames of her lust for Kelly. This made her furious with herself. Why couldn't she just relax and enjoy it all? Why did she have to make everything so hard for herself?

Tony handed her the drink, then ripped the top off a can of beer. "I didn't tell you, did I? — about what happened the other day, when that snooty fashion client arrived for our presentation?"

Laura shook her head, and sipped her drink.

"Well, I thought she must be about due, so I headed 'round to reception. Just as I was about to turn the corner, I saw her standing in the doorway, her mouth hanging open and her eyes like saucers, gaping at Jodie." Tony paused, and lit a cigarette. "She was typing or something and didn't notice the client. Jodie had this huge fucking bubble coming out of her mouth. I reckon it was a personal best — nearly as big as her face!"

Laura laughed. "What did you do?"

Tony took a swig of his beer. "Shit,'mate, I pissed off, back 'round the corner." Laura began laughing hysterically.

Tony dragged on his cigarette calmly. "I waited till I heard this huge fucking snap — the biggest one ever — then I came out and greeted the client, acting as if nothing had happened. I had to try to block her view of Jodie though, who was busy pulling the bloody stuff off her face."

Tony had Laura in fits of laughter, and after a few more drinks, she was in a much better mood.

When she arrived home, she set about putting a meal together to share with Kelly. She made up her mind to relax and enjoy the evening, and the night to follow. Another vodka and tonic would help, she thought, and she sipped this while she prepared a salad of warm poached chicken breast with tomatoes, black olives, capers, and fresh oregano, tossed together with a little lemon juice and olive oil. She opened a bottle of red wine and poured herself a glass, then selected some music. She wondered what Kate was doing tonight and poured another glass of wine.

She was feeling decidedly mellow by the time her door buzzer sounded. She greeted Kelly at the door with one of her smiles. Kelly looked fit and her tan looked great next to her blonde hair. She kissed Laura, a long sensual kiss. Laura was pleased to feel her body respond a little.

When she eventually released Laura, Kelly said with a smile, "Seems like you started without me."

"Yes, I was in the mood," Laura replied. "Come and join me." She took Kelly's hand and led her to the kitchen bench. She was feeling lightheaded as she emptied the bottle into Kelly's glass.

"Shit, you've drunk nearly the whole bottle?" Kelly asked as Laura opened another one.

Laura shrugged. "Well it was nice."

They had dinner and, as expected, Kelly regaled Laura with amusing stories about her trip. At one point, in a break in the conversation, Kelly asked in an off-hand manner, "So have you been seeing your new girlfriend while I've been away?"

Laura felt a sickening grip in her stomach. Frowning, she went into the kitchen. She found her cigarettes and lit one. "That's private. That's got nothing to do with you and me, Kelly," she answered firmly.

Kelly backpedaled fast. "Okay, baby, I'm sorry," she said in a placating tone. "It's none of my business." She got up from the table then and went to Laura in the kitchen. Kissing her neck, she said, "But this is my business. Isn't it?"

Laura was struggling to push thoughts of Kate from her mind. The deceit she felt she was perpetrating seemed worse suddenly when Kelly alluded to Kate.

"Yes," she said in a low voice, "this is your business." Laura began to kiss her, gently at first, but with increasing passion.

"God, I want you baby, let's go to bed," Kelly murmured against Laura's lips.

Kelly's raw sex appeal and Laura's determination were beginning to have the desired effect. But Laura was in no hurry.

"Why don't you make us some coffee while I change the music," she suggested, "then we'll go to bed." She kissed Kelly again.

Across town, Kate was sitting at a bar having a drink with a few friends. They'd had dinner together and had moved on to a women's club. The bar was beginning to fill with dykes and the music was becoming more upbeat. Her friends had settled in for an enjoyable night, but Kate's thoughts kept turning to Laura. She was just thinking how much she was looking forward to seeing Laura tomorrow when she had a wonderful idea. She told her friends that she had something to do, and maybe she'd be back later.

She left the bar, got into her dilapidated old red Mazda, and drove straight to a florist she knew, which stayed open until very late. Once again, she selected a dozen long-stemmed red roses and had them put into a box and tied with a red ribbon. They looked beautiful. Red roses may not be very original, thought Kate, but they were the only flowers special enough for her.

She happily handed over quite a large sum of money, more than she could afford.

Since Laura said she was busy tonight, it was likely she was out somewhere, and Kate decided to leave the flowers for her to find when she came home. If she had visitors, she'd leave them outside her door. But maybe, with any luck, Laura was home by now, alone. In any case, she was sure Laura would be pleased. She didn't want to invade her space, but she wanted Laura to know how much she loved her, and that she was always in her thoughts.

Kate pulled up outside Laura's apartment block at around eleven-fifteen. She looked up to her balcony but couldn't see any light through the French doors, so Laura wasn't at home entertaining friends. She cradled the box of roses. When she got to the security entrance, she hesitated about ringing the buzzer. If she wasn't out somewhere, perhaps she was asleep, and Kate didn't want to wake her. Kate reached into her jeans pocket and grasped the keys to

Laura's apartment, which she'd carried with her every day since their first night together. Laura had obviously forgotten about them and hadn't asked Kate to return them. Kate opened the security door and went inside the foyer. She looked up at the stairs leading to Laura's door and wondered whether she should leave the flowers on the doormat. They'd be safe there, Kate thought. But she smiled as she pictured Laura coming home later, or waking up tomorrow morning, and discovering with delight the spectacular box of flowers on the coffee table. That was a much more exciting idea.

Laura and Kelly were together on the sofa. The music had finished, and the apartment was quiet except for their occasional sighs and moans. They'd been kissing for some time, and Kelly was squirming impatiently. She pressed Laura down onto her back. She slid Laura's sweater up, exposing her breasts, and began to caress Laura's breasts with her lips and tongue.

Laura moved her hips under Kelly and moaned as her own desire increased. "We'd better go upstairs," Laura said breathlessly. She switched off the lamp on the side table, and then with a gaze into Kelly's eyes, took her hand and led her upstairs.

"God, I've missed you," Kelly whispered, as she quickly pulled off Laura's sweater and dragged off her jeans and panties. She removed most of her own clothes and, still in her bra and panties, she drew Laura down onto the bed and began to cover Laura's body with kisses.

* * * * *

Kate began to climb the stairs to Laura's apartment. She hesitated once more, outside her door, listening for sounds of movement. She didn't want to frighten Laura if she was there.

Quietly, Kate placed the key in the lock. She opened the door just a couple of inches, listening. All was quiet, and Kate stepped inside. She closed the door soundlessly behind her and stood for a moment as her eyes adjusted to the darkness. Suddenly, she was aware of a small flickering light coming from upstairs. Kate smiled. It was candlelight. She and Laura often made love by candlelight. Laura must be lying quietly awake, she thought.

Considering whether she should call out to Laura or go outside the door again and knock, she heard a sound. It was a soft moan, and it was Laura's voice. This was followed by another voice, barely audible: "Oh, baby." Kate froze. Her heart began to pound. It couldn't be what it sounded like. It wasn't possible. Some horrible force-field drew Kate unwittingly to the stairs. Her legs felt like jelly and her mind had gone blank. Another murmur, another whisper, and Kate began to slowly ascend the stairs. She was still clutching the box of roses under her arm, but Laura's keys slithered suddenly from her hand, and hit the stair with a loud clang.

Laura and Kelly were lying naked on the bed.

"Fucking hell!" Kelly exclaimed, leaping off Laura in an instant. Laura gasped, grabbing her robe from the end of the bed and clutching it to her naked body.

Kate stared at them in disbelief, and the box

under her arm fell, split open and spilled the red roses over the floor. She suddenly felt sick and, without a word, she turned and fled down the stairs and out of the door.

Upstairs, Kelly had recovered somewhat from the shock of this rude interruption. This wasn't the first time she'd been "caught in the act" by the untimely arrival of a jealous lover. Despite the lightning speed at which it had all taken place, Kelly had noticed the intruder's exceptional good looks and tender age. She smiled, thinking the young woman had just learned the hard way to wait for an invitation next time.

"God, Laura," she called out as she began to descend the stairs. "Don't you know not to give lovers keys to your apartment? That's just a crazy thing to..."

Kelly stopped suddenly. Laura was kneeling on the floor in the open doorway with her robe, having fallen off her shoulders, spread out around her. Her head was down, her face in her hands, and she was sobbing. Kelly pulled Laura to her feet, and pushed the door closed.

"Come on, baby," said Kelly gently. "It's not that bad." She put her arms around her and tried to calm her, but Laura pushed her away.

"It is that bad," Laura sobbed as she rushed to the phone. Breathless and agitated, she left a message with someone. "Please tell her to call me as soon as she gets in."

As Laura put down the phone, and rapidly leafed through her organizer for another number, Kelly said quietly, feeling dejected, "I guess she means a lot to you."

Without turning to look at her, Laura answered thoughtlessly, "Everything."

As Laura dialed another number, Kelly returned to the bedroom and got dressed. When she came back downstairs, she looked at Laura, who was again speaking on the phone. "Good-bye, Laura." Kelly opened the door and left.

CHAPTER THIRTEEN

Laura went into the kitchen and made herself some coffee. Her head was throbbing, and she imagined the agony Kate would be going through. Suddenly, Laura pictured the flowers lying on the bedroom floor, and while the coffee brewed, she went upstairs. She stood for a moment, breathless as she surveyed the bed from Kate's point of view. Crouching down, she slowly gathered up the roses. She didn't feel the pain of a tearing thorn, and she watched in detached interest as the blood welled and trickled across her hand. Returning to the kitchen she placed the roses in a vase and poured herself the first of many cups of coffee.

The hours slowly ticked by as Laura chastised herself for her stupidity. She had to keep moving around, finding things to do, to ease the gripping ache in her chest. She found herself re-living the horror of the day Alex died, and the grief she was feeling for the loss of Kate was not unlike her grief that fateful day five years ago.

In the early hours as a thin gray light began to filter through Laura's windows, a haze lifted from Laura's mind. She could never have Alex again, but here was Kate, offered to her like a gift, and if she lost her now, she would never forgive herself. She remembered that she'd told Kelly that Kate meant "everything" to her, and she realized it was the truth.

By six o'clock, Kate still hadn't called. Laura was exhausted, but sleep was out of the question. She went upstairs, had a long hot shower, then made herself more coffee and something to eat. At seven o'clock, she rang Kate's apartment again, waking her flatmate a second time, only to be told impatiently that Kate hadn't returned. Laura was becoming desperately worried about Kate. Where could she be? Was she all right? If only she could have a chance to hold Kate in her arms and kiss away her tears, assure her that she would never be hurt again. If only she had a chance to tell Kate she loved her. Laura urgently wanted to talk to Jude; she needed her help. They'd planned to meet at the market anyway, but she decided to call sooner.

When she rang her, around eight-thirty, Jude was still sleepy. Laura had woken her. Laura began her story calmly, but within moments, she dissolved in a flood of tears.

Jude was alarmed. "Settle down, darl," she said. "Come around here now, and tell me all about it. We'll sort something out."

After Laura hung up she felt some relief. She washed her face in cold water, then grabbed her keys and mobile phone. Kate knew that number and it was on her answer machine, so she wouldn't miss any calls. Just before she left, she remembered Kelly and decided to phone her. She felt awful about the way she'd ignored her last night.

"Kelly, it's Laura. I've rung to say I'm sorry about last night."

"These things happen, babe," Kelly replied in a casual tone.

"I was very upset . . . obviously, and I ignored you," said Laura. "I wasn't thinking straight, I'm sorry."

"It's okay. You're obviously pretty serious about her. Did you find her?"

"I'm afraid not yet. I'm terribly worried about her," Laura replied.

They agreed to catch up soon, but Laura knew that this ideal affair with Kelly was over.

Laura drove by Kate's apartment on her way, hoping desperately that she might see Kate's car parked outside in its usual place. But it wasn't there. She fought back the tears that threatened to swamp her, and as she continued on to Jude's house, she told herself to remain calm. She had to get a grip on herself and stop being hysterical. But when Jude opened her door later, Laura collapsed on her shoulder in a flood of tears.

After Laura told her the story, Jude said, "Come with me to the market, there's nothing else you can do at the moment. You've got your phone with you just in case." Laura nodded in agreement. "You can spend the day with me if you like, and I'll make a big pot of vegetable soup for dinner. I know you won't eat if you go home."

Laura looked at Jude and smiled. Not for the first time, she considered how lucky she was to have a friend like her. "Thanks, Jude," she replied, "I'd like that."

Kelly had played cricket in the afternoon, and as her team had brilliantly won the match against a formidable, infamous opposition called The Western Deadly Dykes, Kelly and a group of others decided to go out and celebrate. They'd decided after dinner to check out a few clubs. They started with Babes. It was a bit rough and had a reputation for being a sleazy pick-up bar. Kelly didn't like the place much, but it was somewhere to kill a couple of hours. They arrived at around eleven o'clock and settled themselves at the bar. As her eyes adjusted to the dim lights, and her ears adjusted to the loud techno music, Kelly leaned back comfortably on her bar stool, drink in hand, and surveyed the room.

There were a few women lurching about in the semi-darkness, obviously the worse for drink, and a small contingent of energetic dancers on the dance floor. Women at the tables near the dance floor yelled at one other in an attempt at conversation, and huddled couples leaned against the walls in various stages of passionate embrace.

One such couple stood not far from her. She noticed a woman in a white jacket that was glowing brilliantly in the ultra-violet light, leaning over another, who she had pressed against the wall. She was kissing her passionately, and nudging her thigh between the other woman's legs. Kelly watched as the woman in the jacket slipped her hand up under the other woman's sweater and fondled her breasts. Just when Kelly was wondering how far they'd go, they stopped kissing for a moment, and the woman against the wall turned her head.

Kelly's eyes widened in surprise, as she saw it was the beautiful young woman who'd appeared in Laura's apartment last night. It was obvious that she was quite drunk, and was being partly held up against the wall, by the other woman. She watched as once again, the young woman's mouth was smothered in a kiss. Kelly looked away. It wasn't her business. But she recalled the sight of Laura, on the floor last night in tears, distraught, and she knew that Laura wanted to find this girl. It was obvious she wasn't enjoying herself; she was heading for trouble. Kelly sighed and sipped her drink. Letting Laura know where to find this girl wasn't doing herself any favors, she thought. But she cared about Laura, and if she'd fallen in love with this woman, well, it was over with her anyway. Seeing the haunted expression on the girl's face she went out into the foyer, and found the pay-phone.

Babes wasn't far away, and Laura got there in record time. She raced inside the grimy foyer and paused at the counter to pay her nominal entry fee. Impatiently, she waited while a heavily tattooed woman stamped her wrist and slowly looked her over. She walked past the bouncers on the door, and headed for the bar. Kelly turned and looked into her eyes for a moment before indicating, with a nod of her head, where Kate was to be found. Laura kissed her cheek. "Thank you."

Laura moved through the crowd There were women huddled together everywhere. Her eyes had adjusted to the light, and she looked around carefully. Then a woman in a white jacket leaned back a little, revealing the woman she had wrapped in her arms. With a gasp, Laura saw it was Kate. She froze for a moment, when she saw the woman run her hands up under Kate's sweater and begin again to kiss her mouth.

She grabbed Kate's arm. "I have to talk to you," Laura said.

In an exaggerated proprietorial action, the woman began to slowly stroke Kate's back, hips and thighs. Smiling at Laura, she said, "She's busy."

Laura clenched her fists. "Kate!" she said again, looking at her.

"I'll talk to her," Kate said to the woman. "I'll be back in a minute."

Over my dead body, thought Laura as she clasped Kate's hand and led her across the room to a quiet lounge area outside the dance floor. Laura found a table in a dim corner, and they sat down.

Kate looked up at Laura, tossed her hair, and asked coldly, "What do you want to say, Laura?"

Laura wiped at the tears that were running down her face and swallowed hard to clear the lump in her throat. "Baby, I'm so sorry," she began inadequately.

Kate's eyes flashed angrily. "You're sorry! Laura, do you have any idea of how I feel? I was such an idiot to believe in you. All that time, I thought what was happening with us was important and special, but it meant nothing to you. You were still screwing her!" She put her face in her hands to hide her tears.

Laura reached across the table and touched her hair. "Kate, please listen to me."

Kate pulled away from her touch. "You didn't take me seriously, did you? Well maybe you were right! If I wasn't so stupid and inexperienced, I would have known better!"

Just then Laura noticed the skulking figure of the woman in the white jacket hovering nearby. "Is that why you're here? To get experience?"

"Yes!" Kate shouted.

The tears continued to well up in Laura's eyes and spill over. Holding Kate's furious gaze, she said, "I'm in love with you, Kate." There was silence for a moment, while Kate just stared at her in amazement. "I want you to come home with me."

After another pause, Kate asked, "What did you say?"

Laura got up then, went to Kate, and took her into her arms. "I said, I'm in love with you and I want you desperately. Please forgive me, Kate." She felt Kate's body relax in her arms. "I was such a fool, darling. I tried to fight it, but I was in love with you all along." She looked into Kate's eyes. "I want us to be together always. Can you forgive me?"

Kate couldn't speak through her tears. She nodded and Laura stroked Kate's wet cheek.

"I thought I'd lost you, baby. You're more than I deserve. Let's go home." Kate nodded again, and hand in hand they made their way through the throng and left the bar.

EPILOGUE

Jude nearly tripped over a box near the door, and looked around in amazement at the stuff piled around Laura's usually immaculate apartment. Three happy weeks had passed for Kate and Laura, and tonight they were entertaining their first dinner guest.

"Where are you going to fit all this stuff?" Jude asked Laura.

Just then, Kate appeared at the top of the stairs. "In the attic!" Kate replied excitedly. "Come and have a look, it's just been finished."

Jude looked at Laura in surprise. Laura smiled and shrugged. "You better do what the lady says." They both climbed the stairs to join Kate, who led Jude into the large dressing room. A fold-away ladder spilled down from the center of the ceiling.

"My God!" exclaimed Jude, as she followed Kate up the ladder.

The large room under the high gabled roof had a polished floor and built-in cupboards and shelves. There was a pretty dormer window out to the north, and beside it, an easel was supporting one of Kate's half-finished paintings. Empty boxes were lying around.

"This is fabulous! You two have been busy," said Jude, clearly impressed. "This will be Kate's studio," explained Laura, "and a place to store things out of the way. It only took a week to construct, and we did the painting ourselves."

"Who did the painting?" Kate asked with a laugh.

Laura smiled. "Well, you are the painter in the family, darling."

Laura was already dressed for dinner, but Kate was still dressed in an old pair of jeans and a dirty T-shirt. "Come on, let's go downstairs and have a drink," Laura said.

Kate kissed her cheek. "I won't be a minute, I just have to put these things away."

Downstairs, Laura looked at Jude and laughed. "She's so excited about moving in. She's so happy and she just loves the studio."

Jude had brought a bottle of champagne with her to celebrate, and she opened the bottle. "You look extremely happy yourself. I haven't seen you like this for many years."

"I honestly thought I could never feel like this again. I just wish I'd listened to you earlier," Laura said. Just then the cork popped, and Laura grabbed a glass to catch the bubbles. "It was all there for me, and I nearly lost my chance."

Kate ran downstairs to join them. Jude filled the glasses and raised hers in a toast. "To letting go," she said with a knowing smile.

Laura slid her arm around Kate's waist and kissed her cheek. "I'll drink to that!"

ABOUT THE AUTHOR

Ann O'Leary was born in Melbourne, Australia, where she lives in domestic bliss with her partner. After many years working in film production and advertising, she is now a full-time writer. *Letting Go* is Ann's first novel with Naiad Press. *Julia's Song* will be published by Naiad Press in 1998, and *The Other Woman* after that.

A few of the publications of
THE NAIAD PRESS, INC.
P.O. Box 10543 • Tallahassee, Florida 32302
Phone (850) 539-5965
Toll-Free Order Number: 1-800-533-1973
*Mail orders welcome. Please include 15% postage.
Write or call for our free catalog which also features an
incredible selection of lesbian videos.*

OLD BLACK MAGIC by Jaye Maiman. 272 pp. 9th Robin Miller Mystery.	ISBN 1-56280-175-9	$11.95
LEGACY OF LOVE by Marianne K. Martin. 240 pp. Women will do anything for her . . .	ISBN 1-56280-184-8	11.95
LETTING GO by Ann O'Leary. 160 pp. Laura, at 39, in love with 23-year-old Kate.	ISBN 1-56280-183-X	11.95
LADY BE GOOD edited by Barbara Grier and Christine Cassidy. 288 pp. Erotic stories by Naiad Press authors.	ISBN 1-56280-180-5	14.95
CHAIN LETTER by Claire McNab. 288 pp. 9th Carol Ashton mystery.	ISBN 1-56280-181-3	11.95
NIGHT VISION by Laura Adams. 256 pp. Erotic fantasy romance by "famous" author.	ISBN 1-56280-182-1	11.95
SEA TO SHINING SEA by Lisa Shapiro. 256 pp. Unable to resist the raging passion . . .	ISBN 1-56280-177-5	11.95
THIRD DEGREE by Kate Calloway. 224 pp. 3rd Cassidy James mystery.	ISBN 1-56280-185-6	11.95
WHEN THE DANCING STOPS by Therese Szymanski. 272 pp. 1st Brett Higgins mystery.	ISBN 1-56280-186-4	11.95
PHASES OF THE MOON by Julia Watts. 192 pp. . . . . . hungry for everything life has to offer.	ISBN 1-56280-176-7	11.95
BABY IT'S COLD by Jaye Maiman. 256 pp. 5th Robin Miller mystery.	ISBN 1-56280-156-2	10.95

These are just a few of the many Naiad Press titles — we are the oldest and largest lesbian/feminist publishing company in the world. We also offer an enormous selection of lesbian video products. Please request a complete catalog. We offer personal service; we encourage and welcome direct mail orders from individuals who have limited access to bookstores carrying our publications.